OTHER
HEARTBREAKS

STORIES

ALSO BY PATRICIA HENLEY

In the River Sweet

Worship of the Common Heart

Hummingbird House

The Secret of Cartwheels

Friday Night at Silver Star

Backroads

Learning to Die

OTHER
HEARTBREAKS
STORIES

PATRICIA HENLEY

Engine Books
Indianapolis

Engine Books
PO Box 44167
Indianapolis, IN 46244
enginebooks.org

These stories, sometimes in slightly different form, originally appeared in the following journals: *Freight Stories, Glimmer Train, Puerto del Sol, The Normal School,* and *Seattle Review.* "Sun Damage" is published with the permission of MacAdam/Cage. It first appeared in *Worship of the Common Heart.*

The author gratefully acknowledges the support of the College of Liberal Arts and the MFA Program in Creative Writing at Purdue University. She also wishes to thank the Creative Writing Program at the University of Alabama where, for one semester, she held the Coal Royalty Endowed Chair and finished three of these stories.

Also available in eBook formats from Engine Books.

Printed in the United States of America
10   9   8   7   6   5   4   3   2   1

ISBN: 978-0-9835477-2-3
Library of Congress Control Number: 2011932424

FOR MY MOTHER,
VIRGINIA MAE JOHNSON COWGILL

1923-1981

You will always be having to get up from your chairs
To move on to other heartbreaks, be caught in other snares.

JOHN ASHBERY, "Some Words"

CONTENTS

ROCKY GAP

JUNE PECK READS the directions sewn to the new tent. You toss it like a pizza to set it up. And later, inside the tent, she and her sweetie Tanya will watch another episode of *Battlestar Gallactica* on Tanya's laptop, if the battery's juiced.

They drove thirteen hours, Illinois to western Maryland, out of the swelter that everyone says is a sign of global warming. They stopped and bought cowgirl boots—red for June and black for Tanya, embroidered with dragons—and they stopped at Frank Lloyd Wright's Falling Water, where Tanya burst into tears. She said she was moved by it, but June intuits that the house flicked a barb into Tanya's memory. Something June would probably rather not know.

The campsite has a fire pit, a gravel pad for the tent, a greasy picnic table, and an iron hook on which to hang a stuff sack of food to keep it from the bears. And beyond that, the bathhouse, a playground, a lake, where, this particular Thursday in early August, rumor has it that two junior high jokesters—boys—have pooped in the water, and, according to the lifeguard, no one is allowed to swim for two hours, presumably long enough for the matter to disintegrate. There are pin oaks all around. Bikers in do-rags and tattoos. And an open-air arcade where electronic battles seduce the munchkins. June will store their food in the van and she will never, ever, get in the water after that rumor. She has never liked lakes; they're too murky.

It's the first family reunion without her sister Peggy.

The kids, nieces and nephews, are camped at the other end of Elm Loop. She calls them the kids. The oldest is twenty-three and the youngest eighteen. June wants her daughter and grand-daughter—Beth and Miri—next to her. Miri scuffs around in the gravel, intent on the sound her baby sandals make. June doesn't want anyone to feel left out. Underneath that, she thinks: That's their problem if they do. But some people are closer than others. She is closer to Beth and Mike and Miri and Ramsey than she is to anyone. Mike stayed in Ithaca to work on his dissertation; he'll fly in tomorrow and ride back to Ithaca with Beth and Miri. They are a blended family. Mike's son Ramsey is traveling with his mother. Mike's two older children—teenage girls—are white-water rafting in Montana with *their* mother. Mike has these four children with three different women, Beth being the one and only, the last of his red-hot lovers, she likes to say. He fits right in to the family. When Beth told her mother that she had fallen in love with a man with three children, June Peck said, "That makes perfect sense." Beth wanted a family, and Mike gave it to her.

June and not-quite-seven-year-old Ramsey were in the birthing room when Miri was born. Beth was a goddess—that's what June tells everyone. She likes to brag about her.

At that time (the three-year period in which Beth met Mike, married him at a state park on Cayuga Lake, and they had Miri) what Tanya and June had called their relation-space-station was breaking up, fragments scattered in the stratosphere. They'd been in an extended rough patch. Tanya spent a year reading and re-reading a book titled *Yoga and the Search for the True Self.* She said that she was finished with the "identity project" and craved the "reality project."

During Beth's labor, Ramsey was naturally impatient. They played "Go Fish" and "Kings in the Corner." June had taught him to play "Kings in the Corner" when he was five on a Christmas trip to Man O' War Cay in the Bahamas. During the day Tanya and June had held hands, walking the cool December beach. They built labyrinthine sandcastles with Ramsey and marveled at the unsullied genetic make-up of the inhabitants, Tories all. But in the evening there wasn't much to do but play cards and drink gin. On the same trip she taught him to sing "Toot-Toot-Tootsie." They sing it whenever they meet.

At Miri's birth, they were told where to stand. Six feet from the hot spot. Ramsey was at June's hip; he squeezed her hand and said, "You're crying." And June said, "I'm happy. Happy for our family." You can't tell an almost seven-year-old that you've got a broken heart that has nothing to do with what's happening. You can't say that in this labor room are broken hearts, mended hearts, eternal stories of love lost and gained. June couldn't stop trembling. Miri's head swelled out and Ramsey said, "Her head's gigantic!" Later, when the nurse measured Miri in the shallow plastic bassinette, Ramsey said wonderingly to Beth, "It's your first baby." Ramsey seems to get the emotional import of things; he is one of the reasons June wants to live a long life: to see how he turns out.

Beth and Miri are her people and she chose the campsite next to them. She tosses the two-person tent like a pizza and wham-o! They have shelter.

What does she mean when she says that Mike fits right in?

June was married for six months when she was seventeen. He left her for a Vietnamese woman he met during the war. They have three children, and, like a favorite aunt, June is always invited to their birthday parties and graduations. She goes, wanting that connection to the person she was and that time in her life—the sixties. June legally took back her maiden name and cautiously never changed it again. Next came #2, Beth's father, an angry guy she met at the gym. James Hillman writes, in *The Soul's Code,* that sometimes men and women are drawn to each other to make a baby simply so that particular soul may come into being, not necessarily to be lifetime mates. When Tanya told her this, June thought, "There's a newsflash." June gave birth to Beth while married to #2, and then they signed the do-it-yourself divorce papers right before Beth went to first grade. She married again and that lasted eight years. They did some things: climbing mountains and backpacking in the desert. He liked to play military marches on the stereo in the morning. #2 and #3 never contact June, but she did see #2 at Beth's wedding. June considered being cordial to him her spiritual exercise for the month. She had to prep for it.

Then there were those blissful lonely years of living alone in an apartment near the old Carnegie library. Her kitchen had a bay window. The Y was a block away and every other morning she went to the Y and lifted weights. With no one around to question her material urges, she bought pink dishes.

After that, she met Tanya and they decided to have a commitment ceremony. It was her first real wedding. They wore identical cream-colored dresses with lace around the hems of the petticoats, dresses like a fairytale illustration. Now June wishes she'd worn something sexy, a sheath, but with solid infrastructure, Spanx lining, a dress that would remind her that she does indeed have Aphrodite coursing through her veins. Forty years old, she had fallen in love for the first time.

But back to the family's complexity (or quirkiness, oddity, depending on your perspective): June's brother Jimmy from Dayton was a parish priest in an earlier incarnation, but he has been married three times. This one suits him. He has kept his promise to her to quit smoking; she's that good for him. Her sister Anne has been married forever to a man who used to love to bait June with sly sexist comments. She always wonders if he will. He has Johnny Cash on his truck stereo and June slips into what has become their way to get along. They bond over Johnny Cash.

Their sister Peggy died this past March, of liver disease. She was in her late forties, with four children. The youngest of her children lives with Tanya and June. His arrival to their household coincided with the second year of the rough patch.

That winter Tanya was away on a dig in Arizona. June was teaching the boy to drive the rattletrap Ford Ranger that Anne's husband had sold her for a dollar. Now, although June holds the title, he has installed stick-on letters—*24 HOUR HELLRAISER*—across the upper windsheld. The winter Tanya was away, almost every day after school, they went out driving on rural roads. He would considerately tune the radio to a Classic Rock station. June wore sunglasses to hide her tears. But you needed sunglasses that winter—the roads and fallow fields wore ice and snow like a shiny skin. She couldn't seem to control her responses to certain, obvious, songs. "The Thrill is Gone" and "Unchained Melody." After their weekly Habitat for Humanity stint (newbies, they were charged with sweeping frozen gravel and painting the insides of closets), after meatball subs (boy food), after a TV show (*Star Trek* re-runs), they went to bed in separate parts of the house and then June would let loose. That kind of crying—it empties you. She might get up and drink at the kitchen counter, tequila straight up, feeling reckless, even though she had to work the next day. Fool for life, she had not envisioned true love leading to that. *That* being the total reversal of feeling on Tanya's part. It was the sort of winter when ice accretes on the steps and you pour on salt and the salt comes into the house in the Vibram soles of your boots and the parquet floor grows dull from the salt and the photos of the two of you together are put away in a cupboard in the basement. One respite June allowed herself that winter was Italian lessons. Living well is the best revenge: she repeated this daily. Her teacher came to the house on Monday nights. In a wool cape and tall boots, ushering cold into the foyer. She was from Lucca and smelled like familiar cologne. She made June ache for Tanya, so it wasn't all good.

But back to the crazy family: Among the children June's parents had before they passed away from diabetes complications, they can count eight marriages, one commitment ceremony, communal experiments, youthful follies and addictions too numerous to count, moves executed in the middle of the night, bad debts, regret as big as the house they grew up in, and one dead sib. Phantom sib.

Here they are at Rocky Gap State Park, reuniting for three days. Tanya is the one who has said, "Mike fits right in, doesn't he?" Tanya's family is tidy and small. She has one sister, an attorney specializing in outer space law who still lives at home. Secretly June thinks: They wouldn't fart in the bathtub.

Everyone brings firewood for the Holy Moly Dance.

June has imperiously scheduled it for tonight. Peggy's daughter, one of the cousins at the other end of Elm Loop, drives up in a jeep and dumps three bundles of store-bought firewood near the fire pit.

Not everyone came to Peggy's funeral. It wasn't a *funeral* funeral. They called it a memorial service. Her body was kept in cold storage somewhere in the funeral home. There has been some talk of dealing with the ashes, where and when. But no one has made a plan and June hopes they will postpone it. She has to work to suppress memories of Peggy, and those she fails to suppress arise unbidden.

Peggy in a corduroy recliner. Three days after last Christmas. Opaque plastic has been tacked over the windows of her oldest son's cabin. Peggy's jaundiced face is long and gaunt, her hair still black. Her eyes spooky, the skin around them pinched. She knows she is dying. Her legs and feet are swollen, the skin broken open from the swelling. June slathers Gold Bond lotion into her sores. She doesn't want Hospice because you have to declare that you won't seek treatment if you want Hospice to help. (She might ask for a blood transfusion.) A neighbor who works for Hospice has unofficially provided an aluminum walker and after the Gold Bond Peggy clutches the walker and painstakingly clumps her way to the plank porch, which is stacked with firewood. Ice and frozen mud gouge the steep driveway. Fir trees, plaid shirts, the smell of roll-your-own tobacco—when the lid pops off the Bugler can—and a half-lame dog snuffling in a bowl of breakfast leftovers: June's memory works overtime.

A Hospice volunteer left a Living Will and when Peggy comes back indoors, they turn off MTV and go over the Living Will. She wants to be cremated, but before that she would like a CD player and blues CDs. Later June sends her some Little Willie John and Memphis Minnie.

In the summer she always wore a baseball cap.

Her voice was like sandpaper.

Years ago, before she moved to California, she had been assaulted by her husband, her ear nearly torn off. She had assaulted him, too.

When she was a baby her hair was curly, but after her second surgery, it went straight. She was born with a dislocated hip and wore a half-body cast for a year when she was three. June was thirteen and strong enough to carry her in the cast and she was a laughing, dimpled, beautiful baby girl.

She liked to read romances.

Her first baby was born in 1974, when she was sixteen. When

she was newly pregnant she and June and Jimmy drove out west together. They drove up the California coast, camping, eating peanut butter sandwiches. She always liked to say, "Peanut butter tastes best in adverse conditions." Once she stole salami from a Safeway. In San Francisco June tried to talk her into getting an abortion. She never forgave her for that.

What they do in the world:

June is a professor of anthropology at a small state college. After decades she takes it for granted, and whines about the grading, but it is a gift to be a teacher. Willie Nelson writes in his autobiography: "Sixty years ago, if I'd had the opportunity to lay out my life just the way I wanted it to happen—whatever I would have planned would have paled in comparison to what's actually happened. All I can say is, fortunately, I wasn't in control." Proletariat to the bone, not ashamed of Willie, June taped this to her fridge beside a Buddhist saying: "There are few problems that can't be solved by patience." (Liver disease happens to be one of the exceptions. One doctor said, "It's like her liver's Swiss cheese." After the official diagnosis, June asked, "What would you do if she were your sister?" And the doctor said, "I'd get Hospice involved.")

Jimmy is a brilliant alcohol and drug counselor.

Anne is the sort of devoted mother who sewed clothes for her children when they were toddlers. A throwback to their Czech aunts who made Easter dresses with big sashes and hair-bows to match. June sometimes thinks to herself that Anne did everything right; she didn't consider her own needs until her nest was empty. Now she line-dances once a week at Neon Cactus in Cincinnati. In the fall she'll start massage therapy classes.

Peggy is dead.

Miri and June go for a walk while everyone cooks. Miri turned two in March and thinks she knows the makes of cars and trucks. Beside a rear tire on the Town and Country van June rented for the trip, Miri squats, plucks her passy out of her mouth, and with authority she says, "BMW." This gets a big laugh from everyone who has ever coveted a BMW. She spots an enormous red truck and says, "Chevy." June says, "Ford." Her hand in June's is sweet, still a surprise, windfall.

Later, after the salmon and salads, after carrot cake, the night feels like something viscous. At June and Tanya's site, a fire rises, stick by stick, hunk by hunk.

They toss little scraps of origami wishes into the fire. June thinks that she should wish for World Peace, but she doesn't. She wishes for Local Peace. That is, she wishes for constancy with Tanya. June is ready for change. Ready for bells ringing, blossom, sunshine, the hand of a loved one in hers. Try a little tenderness, that's what she's ready for.

Then they chant: holy moly holy moly holy moly holy moly holy moly holy moly holy moly holy moly holy moly holy moly holy moly holy moly holy moly holy moly holy moly holy moly holy moly holy moly holy moly. Drummers drum, tablas and bongos. Voices fly, shimmer into trees; percussive clapping ascends. And the yipping and high-pitched hollers and wails. A little drunk so early, Anne's husband bows deeply, his gray hair flopping, and on the upswing he bellows, "Can I get a *wit*ness?" The children stand spellbound and Miri is in her mother's arms and their faces are cast in the glint and flicker of golden flames. Tanya whispers: "Will this be Miri's first memory?"

Tanya is the only woman to jump over the fire. She is young, athletic, deliciously show-offy. One of Jimmy's ex-wives—Dee-Dee, the gorgeous—drives up, music trickling from her car stereo. She hops out, waves her arms, and bawls, "Hello, heathens." But after a few minutes, she and Tanya stroll to the bathhouse together. As if they had planned it. There was a time when June might have felt a little buzz of romantic anxiety, her beloved walking into the full-moon dark with another woman, but now that the worst that can happen in love has happened, she is past fear. This is the good that came out of the rough patch: cornerstone of the reality project.

When the chanting dies down, Miri bats a fist against her thigh, squealing, "Do *again*, do *again*."

*   *   *

Starting with childhood, June's addictions have included junk novels, bakery products (she can still sniff out a ma-and-pa doughnut shop peripherally in any town), black beauties obtained with forged prescriptions, cigarettes, white sugar, exercise, and espresso. All uppers. Had her drug of choice been alcohol, she doesn't know if she could have stopped. She might have ended up where Peggy did. Huddled under an electric blanket in an unheated trailer in a town over two thousand miles from family. Her liver shot.

Her daughter kept calling them from Mendocino. "My mother's dying. She won't go to the doctor."

That was right after Thanksgiving last year. They called each other, a net of telephone calls, criss-crossing the country, and they called Peggy, but she would not pick up.

June consulted daily with Jimmy, sometimes three or four times. They had been closest to her and they became mission control. Jimmy said that the police anywhere will do a security check on someone you're worried about. June had forgotten this. But a long time ago when she and Jimmy lived in a commune in North Carolina and Jimmy was only sixteen, their parents sent the sheriff out to check on him—an alarming event for everyone with sheaves of dope drying in the rafters, alongside the chamomile and borage.

So they asked the police to check on Peggy. She refused to answer the door and they meekly went away. It was the rainy season in Mendocino. June could imagine the cold rain, the police standing on the postage-stamp porch in the slanting rain, banging on the aluminum screen door, Peggy in the back bedroom under the electric blanket, shivering. Did she get up and check the door when they left? Did she turn on the TV and watch the soaps? Did she ever think of her brother and sisters? Did she remember June carrying her in the body cast when she was a baby girl? Did she remember the blackberries they picked? Did she ever look at those Catholic school pictures of herself in a red plaid dress, grinning irrepressibly, with coal black braids? Did she relive that phone call when she entrusted her boy to June and Tanya?

Next, they sent her oldest son to Mendocino. He flew out from Dulles and within a couple days he convinced Peggy to go to the hospital. She was given a blood transfusion. With alcoholism at this stage, you develop varicose veins in your stomach and you bleed internally. If you're given a blood transfusion, you perk up. A palliative measure only, the doctors warned them. There was a nice woman doctor. She was the one who gave them the Swiss cheese diagnosis, the one who told June to get Hospice involved. Remembering it like this, everything seems to have an orderly progression, but there were exhausting phone calls to strangers, tidbits of information, a puzzle to construct. It felt to June that decisions needed to be made, but who was to make them? Could Peggy? When the body refuses to process potassium the brain refuses to function reasonably and she would fade in and out and she would forget from one hour to the next what they had discussed.

Finally a nursing home seemed like the sensible option. They were told there might not be a bed for her in Mendocino. She might be sent as far away as the Bay Area. Her daughter was the only family she had in California. Who would visit her in a nursing home in the Bay Area?

Around the first of December June became convinced that Peggy should return to Maryland, and she campaigned for that. (Tanya wasn't so sure. Tanya stayed out of the way; she spent time in Evanston with her tidy, small family. That was a relief to her, June suspects, a manageable family.) Peggy's oldest son stepped up. He said that she should come and live with him and his wife and baby girl in Maryland. She would have to be transported to Sacramento and she would have to fly across the country to Pittsburgh and then be driven to Deep Creek Lake, where she grew up. The nice woman doctor ordered another transfusion and released her. The hospital couldn't keep her there any longer: she was indigent. They tracked her progress across America via cell phone. Moving her into her son's cabin up the steep hill was a job that took three men.

What June said several times to Tanya was this: She hasn't had a life with much dignity. I'd like her to die with dignity.

Once, years ago, June and Tanya had gone to visit Peggy in Mendocino. She and the children were living in a concrete block shell, an abandoned motel. Tanya took the children to an arcade while June took Peggy out for lunch. They sat outdoors in plastic chairs, with water—a lake or pond, June can't remember—visible in the distance. Gulls glided on the breeze, carrying off scattered bits of hamburger buns. Finally June broached the unspeakable— her drinking. Peggy shoved the flimsy table and lit a cigarette. "Save your breath. I don't want to talk about it."

Talking to a drunk about drinking is like talking to a stranger about slapping her children at the mall. You figure: there's something terribly wrong here, but do I have the right to say so?

There was one other time June faced it head-on. She and Tanya had bought a new house, but they were having trouble selling their old house. It was on the flood plain. According to federal flood insurance regulations, they were not allowed to add on to it, but they had remodeled the bathroom and winterized the sun porch. Mature trees grew on the lot and a creek, a tributary of the Kankakee, dallied across the back. They decided to offer the house to Peggy. They would continue to pay the mortgage and Peggy could live in the house rent-free. June could picture it. They would all move from California to Illinois. She and Tanya would take the children to Wrigley Field; they would help them with homework. Their only stipulation was this: Peggy had to quit drinking. She said no, thanks, and hung up.

After that June focused on the children.

At the reunion six years ago at Hueston Woods in Ohio, Peggy's daughter told June, "My mother has liver disease. She's going to die." June went for a walk with Peggy and asked if that were true. "She lies," she said. "You can't believe everything she says."

Since their parents passed away in the eighties, they have had four family reunions.

Elk Neck. Lost River. Hueston Woods. And now, Rocky Gap. They speak of these reunions as if they were summits. The Pecks are convinced that they have a special fate. They survived their parents' excess, their imprudence, their disorganization, their inability to harness their darkest energy. That generation, they didn't know much more about psychology than people who lived during the Civil War. They were both drinkers and gamblers. Winter nights, the sound of them fighting was a hot brand on your heart.

Some forks in the road no one knows about but the two people involved.

There were phone calls from a shelter for battered women. Peggy did not know where to go. She had no money. She had three children still at home; the oldest was in the Army. Her husband had nearly torn off her ear. It had been three years since June's commitment ceremony with Tanya. Her tenure year was over. Beth had graduated from college and was on her own (although later she would decide to go to graduate school and she successfully defended her dissertation this past April and June was there with a bottle of champagne). For a brief time June gloried in the feeling of financial freedom. Tanya and she were both savers. There were no grandchildren. They planned a tour of Tanzania to see the big animals and they planned decadent getaways to Chicago. It was the start of June's sabbatical. About the house, they had installed elegant ceiling fans and bought a stainless steel fridge and a new furnace.

When Peggy called from the battered women's shelter in Morgantown, June silently resisted her. She could not say, "Why don't you come here?" The words stuck in her throat. And who is to say Peggy would have come? Instead, June said, "Where do you want to go?" And Peggy said, in that raspy voice, blowing cigarette smoke away from the receiver, "As far away from him as possible." And June said, "Do you know anyone far away who could help you get settled?" She said she would think about it. The next day she called collect and said that she had a friend in Mendocino, another single mother, and she wanted to move to California. Tanya and June sent her four Amtrak tickets and she moved to Mendocino.

That is the telephone conversation June usually suppresses. Ten years ago there was that moment when she might have said, "Come here," and didn't. Ruthless, aloof, she was headed to San Miguel de Allende on sabbatical, her luggage packed. Tell me what I want to hear: Peggy got the message. She invented California as her destination.

For her memorial service, they arranged the showy zinnias and carnations, which her daughter said Peggy loved. They stationed photographs of her on short wooden pillars among the flowers at the funeral home. Peggy as a young mother in shorts and T-shirt, her four children gathered around her in a summer yard. A kindergartner, with those frayed black braids and that red plaid dress. In a cap and gown, with friends, at her graduation from a junior college, a feat she accomplished during a two-year period of sobriety, with babies underfoot.

At the funeral home, her children sat tearfully in the front row. One was in the Air Force and the Red Cross flew him to Maryland from Kurdistan. One was a young father. One (June's) was still in high school. And her only daughter, twenty-two, was a firecracker, a hard worker, in training to be a loan officer at a bank.

Jimmy wrote a statement and asked June if she would read it at the service. She agreed. First, she told a story about a woman she had met at a conference who does solo trips in the Alaska backcountry. A helicopter drops her off in an undulating field of bear grass and picks her up a month later. June had said, "What's it like coming back to civilization?" And June had an answer already—she thought there could only *be* one answer: that the woman was disgusted with the traffic and the glare, the anxiety and the commerce. But this woman told June: "I am always so touched by the kindnesses people pay one another. Even people who might never meet again—they do the kindest things." June freely wept. She said, "That's what I'll always remember about the last few months. How kind we were to each other and to Peggy." Then she read what Jimmy wrote.

When Peggy was a young girl she had hip surgery and she had to wear a body cast. For over a year of her young life, she was unable to walk, run, play or do much of anything for herself. In some respects, I'm not sure she was ever able to completely break free of that cast; many of her dreams and aspirations remain unfulfilled. We can be hopeful that she is now released. Free of the pain and frustration found in this world, she is released.

As we remember Peggy, I'm sure she would like me to remind you of her love of baseball. Let's not forget and let's carry forward her love of baseball and the New York Yankees. I'm sorry she did not quite make it to opening day.

As we comfort each other here today and in the future, let's cling fast to our fond memories of Peggy, and not dwell on any disappointments, any regret of things that might have been, things that we cannot change. Release those regrets. Let's carry forward our memory of Peggy's idealism, her generous spirit, her love for her children and her brother and sisters, and her courage.

June could see the part in Peggy's daughter's red hair. She sobbed into her own lap. That was the sound of true sobbing. Like Peggy's on the day she agreed that her youngest son should live with June and Tanya. The day she relinquished what her life had been, for what it was to become: waiting to die.

At the funeral home, June did not think of the talk at the dining room table two nights before. How Peggy had let the children run dangerously wild and someone had called Child Protective Services. How the liquor bottles had piled up in the kitchen. How she had thrown teenage tantrums when their mother was still alive, kicking and screaming on the linoleum floor of the house in Deer Park. How she had left dishes in the sink in Mendocino until mold was like fur over everything. How she *was*: irrational, selfish, manipulative, thoughtless. They had to get all that out of their systems. They tried to. They laughed about some of it. June couldn't help but think how close she had come to being Peggy. All that drinking she did in grad school; all that acid she dropped; all the times she put her own stupid desires above Beth's needs. Taking care of Peggy's children is her atonement.

When June was on sabbatical in San Miguel, Peggy would call

her. In the pasture next to the tavern she frequented, a miniature horse had been born. Peggy told her about the horse as if it were hers. Clearly good news. June listened on the clunky black Mexican rotary phone from yesteryear. It was almost as if they were old friends. But they weren't. June couldn't hear her voice without thinking: What does she want now?

For Elk Neck in 1999, Jimmy burned the entire life of their family onto a CD. Dazed Czech women behind a tenement in Chicago, a year since they'd set foot on Ellis Island. June, pregnant with Beth, in a red bandana-print top. Their mother in 1944, a WAC on a forklift, her cap jaunty. Honorable discharges. Report cards from 1929. Photos of their grandfather in front of The Dixie Bee Garage. In the late fifties, kids without their shirts in summer. They got into plenty of trouble. Setting field fires. Grinning innocently. They *were* innocent. Six miles from town, with only network TV.

Holy Moly is over; people have wandered on to other campsites. Her headlamp glowing, June is testing the elastic guy cords on the new tent. Tanya sidles up to June and says, "I talked to Dee-Dee about Peggy."

"And?"

"Don't take it wrong. What she said helped."

"What'd she say?"

"She said, 'Someone in your family has to die first.'"

Someone may beg to be released from pain with morphine.

Someone may suffer head injuries in a car crash.

Some fortunate one might keel over in a vegetable garden from heatstroke. This has been known to happen in their old country family. They were big-time gardeners.

Kohlrabi and cauliflower people.

The last sib will have to watch it, and scatter ashes. Or ride in a car behind the hearse, to and fro.

For now, this is August, at Rocky Gap. June wants to sing "Peg o' My Heart" to Miri the way their mother did. After one verse,

Miri will say, "Do *again*." June and Tanya are getting along and that makes her feel like singing. She wishes she could turn to Peggy as she lifts another beer from the cooler. "Tell me again," she'd say, "how you made friends with that little horse. How he licked the molasses from your palm."

# RED LILY

FATHER BILL HAD BEEN SENT AWAY. There was a home for them in South Carolina, her mother said, a place where they could straighten out. Jenny wondered if there were bars on the windows. It happened almost overnight. He presided at Mass on Ash Wednesday, and the next morning they saw him two doors down at the brownstone rectory, scraping ice off his windshield with the edge of a plastic cassette case. Then into the car went two suitcases and a stack of books. He did not look back. Hypocrites, her mother said, and she stopped going, even though she kept her part-time job selling rosaries and holy cards at Catholic Supply in the church basement. Jenny went ahead and made her first confession and communion that year. She never got over the allure of confession, the dusty maroon curtain, the whispers and stories, the buoyant relief, saying her penance at the communion rail, having been absolved of her childish sins, little lies and selfishness.

Her father moved out a year later. The Wabash had flooded. She had been afraid of the river water swirling around the tires. Leaning out the window of the station wagon. They had been to the zoo and eaten frozen custard—it was the first day of frozen custard season, which was really ice cream. Frozen custard had been outlawed, but the sign stayed the same, a polar bear dancing a jig. Her father let her get out of the car and pick her way to the house around the smelly puddles on the sidewalk before he gunned the engine and disappeared out of town, her mother said, and across the state line, to Ohio. These memories were folded in with others from that turbulent time: Waverly coming to live upstairs for the rent money; her grandfather's heart attack and the funeral where she had glimpsed the men drinking from a brown bottle in a back room of the funeral parlor on Ferry Street; her mother saying, "No more church. No more confession. No more fish on Friday. Promise me you'll never go."

Then things calmed down. Jenny became a gatherer of secrets, a gossip. These morsels she brought to her mother every evening for twenty-five years, always the sins of others, never her own. As she grew up, if ever guilt nagged at her, she would think, How could it be gossip if people told on themselves?

Jenny sometimes spied curiously on the weddings or funerals spilling out on the limestone steps of the church, both occasions appearing similar to the casual observer, with well-wishers or mourners dressed in pinstripe suits and lace-trimmed navy-blue dresses squared off with shoulder pads. At Catholic Supply her mother's boss was now Father Rickie; they would see him in the summertime, cooking over an hibachi on the widow's walk of the rectory. Jenny sometimes daydreamed about the confessional. She stopped in front of the church and memorized the Mass and reconciliation schedule, thinking, Someday. Her sins were backlogged, a clerical mess. They seemed to infect her like particular strains of the flu. Spite was big the winter her mother and Waverly got together, the same year Eddie Fox and Sharla got together. Spite and jealousy and meanness.

At the last Halloween party, Sharla had come dressed as the boss, His Honor, head of English, in an olive-drab trench coat and wing-tip shoes that had probably belonged to a dead man, purchased at the Goodwill for one dollar. The secretaries always made fun of him. A fashion plate in his early forties, he wore his black hair shaggy like a seventies rock star, and he smelled of pipe tobacco and garlic, which he believed to have curative powers. His wife had gone to Oregon to care for her ailing parents and never returned. He finally divorced her, but not bitterly. Sharla was not his secretary, Jenny was. He wanted to remarry, he had confided when

Jenny saw him packing up family photos to take home. He didn't want reminders of his ex around. There were no children to keep up appearances for. Jenny imagined that he wanted children and sometimes she pictured bringing a baby home to him. Wrapped in a pastel receiving blanket. A boy with a mass of black hair. All the steps before that, leading up to a baby, were foggy. Only staff and junior faculty attended the Halloween bash; Sharla's costume was a secret amongst them. As the night wore on, she'd opened the trench coat like a flasher and shown them her lace teddy. The lights had been dim; you couldn't see everything. She'd been a little drunk on mimosas and Eddie had taken her home. Jenny had laughed as loudly as anyone when Sharla flashed open the trench coat. She wanted to be part of it all, but she decided right then to edge Sharla out.

Before Tarkington College, Jenny Rogers had worked selling services—Chem-Dry carpet cleaning, septic tank pumping, landscaping, efforts at tidiness, wholesomeness, and beauty. In a cement block building on the edge of a nearly abandoned industrial park, she would sit in a padded cubicle under skim-milky florescence, a headset on to leave her hands free, and she took orders, usually from women. She would wonder what their houses were like. Jumbles of toys and inherited knick-knacks, or streamlined, maple and stainless steel, with what she still called under-the-counter dishwashers—she and her mother had never had one. She envied the men who went out on the jobs. They smelled the house smells—lemon oil or perfume or baby powder—while Jenny was stuck with a magazine picture of Lake Michigan in winter tacked to her cubicle wall. But she had escaped that life. She had been at Tarkington College for nearly eleven years, a hunger satisfied.

She had her own office, attached to His Honor's, with doors she could shut if she wanted to listen to a love song on the radio turned low or if she wanted a good cry—that had happened only twice, but she liked knowing a modicum of privacy was possible. Her office had a window—not all did—and many admired her view: a brick patio surrounded by river birches and yellow tulips that bloomed in April. Sharla in the main office received everyone—Fed Ex delivery, students, faculty, spouses of faculty with new babies to show off. Gayleen spent her days in the eight-by-fifteen photocopy room across the hall. They called the head His Honor behind his back. Keep the kid gloves handy, Jenny would say, he was one to tiptoe around. You never knew when he might jab you with a smart remark. Several mornings a week he worked at home on a book some people said he'd been writing for ten years, a book about theory, she'd been told, what wasn't real, just an idea, Jenny translated. During his mornings at home she took visitors. Students and faculty would stop by, discreetly checking to see if His Honor was out. They would lean in her doorway or perch on the library chair which she'd dressed up with a kitchen chair pad printed with pink toasters and tea cups. They might say, "Cute as a button," at the photo of her tortoise shell cat—Jellybean. Or they might bring her bags of zucchini from their gardens.

She would get the lowdown.

Sooner or later, everyone told secrets.

She knew that after the league games at Star Lanes, the men on the bowling team went to the Lingerie Demonstrations out on State Highway 23.

She knew the reproductive history of everyone, when pregnancy scares occurred, when pregnancy tests were taken, when miscarriages and abortions were buried in the souls of would-be mothers.

She waited for CAT-scan results.

She knew about lumps and suspicious moles.

She loaned small sums of money to needy students.

She knew when professors were canceling classes to go for job interviews at more prestigious institutions. You wouldn't have to go far for that. The course load at Tarkington was four/four. The class cap was thirty-five.

And the affairs of the heart, the field of sexual energy surrounding people who were smitten or people who had met at the wrong time, wrong place, who were married or committed to others—she had radar for that.

Students said she was a surrogate mother. At those moments, an inner voice nearly squealed at her. Lighten your hair! Get a tattoo! Buy velour tights! Still, she didn't take offense, even though she was only thirty-two. It was something to hide behind.

All winter Jenny plotted to make Sharla look bad. The holidays were an excuse for frivolity, for trays of iced cookies brought in for general consumption and personal leave time extended for shopping. It was easy to blame Sharla for a job not quite completed; Jenny did not have to lie; she merely pointed out with a shrug and a wince what would have been ignored any other Christmas. Later, in the new year, she stayed after hours and on Sharla's hard drive she made a slight change in the grammar of a congratulatory form letter to parents of star students. The letter went out without additional proofing and a senior wrote a snotty editorial for the school paper about the poor grammar. A message Sharla had taken was misplaced, torn into tiny pink shreds and flushed down the toilet. Jenny said to His Honor, "I'll have to keep an eye on her." "Please, Jen," he said, with a long-suffering roll of his eyes. She kept tabs on Sharla's tardiness and reported it, exaggerated it, slipping in musingly, "She might not work out." "You're right about that," he said. "I'll have a talk with her."

Sharla was called in. A compact, determined woman in her mid-twenties with a ruddy, pugnacious face, she sat in Jenny's office, nervously eyeing His Honor's door, picking at the appliqué on her felt skirt. You couldn't remember the color of her hair unless she was right in front of you: linoleum brown. Jenny knew his style; His Honor could put the fear of God in you without being specific. Sharla came out contrite and slunk around the building ashamed for a few days. It was only a matter of time, Jenny self-righteously told her mother when she reported the incidents. She nearly came to believe in Sharla's laxity herself, losing track of what Sharla had done or not done, losing track of truth in the flushed, almost sexual feeling she had when she was about to sneak around or tattle.

* * *

Eddie Fox, who taught geology, had a job offer in Florida. He closed Jenny's office door for privacy on a blustery Friday in February, the week before Ash Wednesday. She didn't think of it that way at the time—the week before Ash Wednesday—but later she would. Students darted beneath her window, their umbrellas blown inside out by a wild gust. Eddie's cowboy boots turned up at the toes. He wore jeans so smooth they might still be iron-hot to the touch, a white dress shirt, a barn jacket waterproofed with wax. His clean-shaven face was long and scarred from acne along one cheek, a scar the shape of a river's oxbow. She had watched his strawberry blond hairline recede, but he was the sort of man who joked about it.

Jenny knew every inch of Eddie; she could bring him forth anytime, anywhere. Thoughts of him could make her feverish with want; she could pass an hour lying on a sofa, sick with desire for him, the way you feel when you've eaten too much store-bought cake.

"What about Sharla?" Jenny said. She felt tears about to come. A ballad on the radio fueled her sadness.

"We never, you know, made a commitment." Eddie opened a candy jar and plucked out a miniature chocolate bar, unwrapped it, and popped it into his mouth. She wished he hadn't said that. She didn't want to know with what indifference he shrugged off Sharla, in spite of her wish for Sharla to die, disappear, or quit.

A pro-forma knock interrupted them—she was about to say, Come off it, Eddie. Sharla and Gayleen squeezed into the office.

Gayleen was a wisp, blond, a chatterbox, always in black, fresh out of junior college.

Smart as a whip, Eddie had said about Sharla, and for some reason that phrase stuck with Jenny and she resented it every time she was in the presence of Eddie and Sharla at the same time. Jenny didn't need to be told that. Sharla took the free course every year and she paid for two more. She had thirty credits. The handbags she collected reminded Jenny of sewing baskets. She went to Indy monthly to buy vintage clothes, red sweater sets from the fifties and poodle skirts.

Eddie excused himself, smilingly. "Got to go, got to go, ladies." On the way out, he patted Sharla's knee; she smiled like the

Mona Lisa. Jenny could read her a mile away: she was at his mercy.

"Well?" Jenny said.

"He'll be in Tallahassee," Sharla said, averting her gaze. "I don't really care, Jen. I never want to get married. Marriage breaks your backbone."

Jenny showed them a find from the prior weekend, a stiff black-and-white photograph of a white-haired man in a casket surrounded by rose wreaths. She collected antique funeral photos. Sharla showed them her bracelet made from old buttons, fake ivory and rhinestone. Gayleen suffered these exchanges restlessly, snapping her fingers, wiggling in an abbreviated dance to the classic rock on the radio. Finally she said, "Cabin fever, that's what I've got."

She and Sharla left as unceremoniously as they had arrived. They were doing their rounds while His Honor was at a meeting; Jenny would never do that. She was a good girl, her mother said. His Honor had praised her at her annual review; she was doggedly responsible, to force him to praise her. Gayleen would not last long at Tarkington, in Jenny's opinion. All on her own, she would sabotage the job. She was late more than not, and whined about the work assigned. She talked about moving to Bloomington where covens practiced white magic in public parks. "They want to cast off restraint, Jenny. No guilt."

Gayleen had been the source of news regarding Eddie and Sharla, and what Sharla and Eddie thought of marriage had been a predominant theme. Once a week all winter Jenny had accompanied Gayleen on her smoking jaunts to the south steps of the building where they might with luck find diluted sunshine; they would stand in wool coats and scarves, gossiping, while Gayleen smoked a filterless cigarette. To mark the hour, the mechanical bells in the tower chimed "The Way We Were."

"It's been going on since summer—you must've known," Gayleen had said, the first time the topic was broached. "They went to the dunes together."

"The dunes?"

"Haven't you been anywhere?"

"I've been to Wyoming," Jenny said.

"What for?"

"My cousin out there had twins. I went out to help her. Before Chem-Dry. I rode the Greyhound to Gillette and saw antelope in the fields." She rarely thought about the cousin now, the sweet-poop odor of the babies, their bleating, but the experience had altered her view of motherhood and what it might demand of you. She had decided then it wasn't worth it. Now she thought babies might be your passion. At campus picnics the babies charmed her. She felt voluptuous and competent in their presence.

"Well, the dunes are only two hours from here, if you don't mind speeding."

"We didn't get that far when I took Roadside Geology from him."

"They still use condoms."

"What difference does that make?"

Gayleen, for her age, had esoteric knowledge about the nuances of relationship. "It just tells me," she said, "they're not that committed. Or she'd get the pill. They have the kind of commitment where you don't have to talk every day. It's a level you get to. Some never get past it."

Jenny had never considered such stages of commitment. She didn't know what to expect, but as they talked, over the winter, she knew she did still expect something. Some flood—of desire or care—that would become bedrock. In her mind, the process didn't take much time, but it might be more geologic.

The day before Eddie's announcement about moving to Tallahassee, she had said to Gayleen, "Do you believe in love at first sight?"

"My mother says that's an old wife's tale."

"My mother says, 'Love's slavery, girl.'"

She said that, but Jenny could not rely on her mother now. Ever since Thanksgiving her mother and Waverly had been doing it right under her nose. He had carved the turkey. He had called her Mary Helen, what no one had called her mother since high school. She usually went by Suzie-Q, the nickname given her by her brother. How did Waverly know about Mary Helen?

Gayleen had smirked. "That's a bad attitude, Jenny. You'll never find a hubby." Her voice rose cynically on the word *hubby*.

She bent over and smashed her cigarette butt on the concrete. "Come to Cox's Pub with us. Karaoke's fun, Jen. You lose your inhibitions."

Jenny always begged off. She couldn't imagine getting up on stage with young people and making a fool of herself. Inhibitions were God-given, her mother always warned.

The day of Eddie's announcement, she didn't want to go home. He'd left her feeling bereft. It was the loss of a fantasy—she was self-aware enough to see that. At home she would have to put up with Waverly. He had been there every evening for a week. She never told her mother the stories with Waverly there. Her mother would usually have supper on the table. The Christmas tree would be lit in the window, no matter the season. In 1967 her mother's brother had died in Vietnam two days before Christmas and the tree had been lit ever since. They had replaced the original aluminum tree and the light bulbs had blinked out now and again and been replenished. It was a commitment her grandfather had made and when he passed away, the obligation fell to Jenny's mother.

There was always a smell in the house—an electric smell, as if wiring might melt at any moment, and also cigarette butts too long in the ashtray—her mother's menthols. Thin and brittle, with a mouth wrinkled and soured by smoking, she was given to wearing loose pants and tunics that might have been pajamas, but she wore them to the supermarket and the convenience store on the next block where she purchased cigarettes and Nirvana Cash lottery tickets. Jenny felt an aversive tug away from the house whenever she imagined Waverly kissing that sour mouth. The odor of whatever her mother had cooked would waft over everything, often meat and onions and potatoes in one form or another. She had a cookbook called *The Perfect Potato.*

Upstairs Waverly would have left MTV throbbing, as if he had only come down for a moment. For a while when she was still in high school, Waverly had been the one Jenny secretly wanted. He drove a delivery truck for Coca-Cola, and after work she would try to catch him in the yard, tending what he'd planted—Scotch bells and lilies and pinks.

There was always someone she wanted, someone impossible. She had not been interested in the garden; in fact, she had a mild fear she kept to herself, a fear of dirty hands, and she washed hers more often than necessary.

She went home anyway; there was no place else to go. She got out of her shoes and into house slippers left by the door in winter. Waverly said, "What's up?" And her mother said, "We're going to add a deck this spring." She fanned brochures on the table, pictures of people in shorts and sundresses, lounging on a white deck that blazed in the sun. They ate dinner together, with Waverly pinching tiny bits of food and feeding them to Jellybean, who begged. Jenny pushed her food around on the plate, unable to eat.

It felt as if her mother were unfaithful to something. But to what? The life they had led. The sameness. Jenny had done whatever her mother said to do, and this was her reward. She tried not to think about Waverly's body against her mother's body. It was too rough, too shameful. They were doing it. She was sure of that. Sex was what they could not mention, with him there, but it lay there intangibly on the table. He might be waiting for Jenny to go to her room to reach out, to say something vulgar. Gayleen had told her that lovers are vulgar, like children spouting dirty words. She thought that she might trade rooms with Waverly. Or run away.

"I might go to church," Jenny said.

"Jen."

"I might." The thought had been surfacing for a while, like a fish coming up out of water to snag insects. Still, she surprised herself.

"No harm in that," Waverly said.

So her mother hadn't told him everything. There were still some things he didn't know. She wondered when they had started up. When was that moment when they first really looked at each other? Waverly must have been fifteen years younger than her mother. He chewed his fingernails down to the quick and they were unsightly, almost obscene. He always wore a Harley-Davidson neckerchief. If she got close to him, he smelled yeasty, like beer.

"You don't know anything about it," Jenny said, her voice

quavering. What she felt had so little to do with them; it was all about Eddie Fox.

Waverly shrugged and pulled Jellybean onto his lap and stroked him. The strokes were long and generous.

She got up and went into her room, gathering her purse, her shoes, as if she had all the time in the world. She put on her special Italian shoes, a find at the AIDS consignment store—suede the color of limes. Gayleen had said they probably had at one time belonged to a drag queen with fake fingernails to match. She didn't care. She wanted it to be special, for she hadn't been to confession in over twenty years. When she came out, they were clearing the table. No one said a word. She flung on her coat and hat. She stood in the foyer and pulled on her gloves. She wondered what life was like where Eddie was headed, Tallahassee or a Caribbean island. People there weren't pulling on gloves in February. There were places where people listened to music outdoors, where they drank tropical drinks and barbecued whole pigs. Loyalties were not secure in places like that. People ran off on boats with strangers. Women wore thongs. Inhibitions were considered old-fashioned, out of the last century. Or the one before that. She could never go. She could never figure out how. One time she had known what that felt like. Only once. What kind of roadside geology would you find there? Wouldn't Eddie miss the moraines?

She was just in time. The church felt forbidden. They didn't hold confession as they had when she was a girl, with the dusty curtain between you and the priest, the anonymity, the halting whispers and sweaty palms. The church lights were dimmed, and the four confessors came in solemn pairs up the aisle in white robes. After an entrance chant, a prayer, the priests—even the Bishop had come—took to their corners, pre-arranged positions here and there around the church. The penitents went like spokes in a wheel to them, and the church was filled with the consistent hum of sin. Jenny went to the back of Father Rickie's line. She wanted to be last.

Her hands shook. He was a few years older than she, but Father Rickie seemed young up close, like someone's little brother. Did he even shave? She heard her mother's voice: They're hypocrites. As if that were the worst you could be.

A small sin might be a good way to begin: a misdemeanor, selfishness, the habit she had of always saving the heels of the bread for herself, for she felt they were a luxury, and her mother thought so, too. Then she would build up to a larger selfishness, how she had not wanted to see her mother's need. How she had controlled her mother. I'll be good if you'll be good. Until now.

But instead of the small sin, she blurted out, "He showed me the rocks, Father, in the lab storage room. He expected me to help him move them. Just because, I imagine, I work for the college. This would be after hours. We were alone in the building. It's the one way out by the physical plant—"

Father Rickie glanced around. "You might want to lower your voice." He smiled tentatively, encouragingly.

She tried to be cooperative. She had not anticipated the pleasure in telling her story, the way she had the opportunity to relive it, the bad parts as well as the good. "He had a big chunk of obsidian in there. Beautiful, black. Glassy. He'd found it himself, he said. He stood so close. I could hear him breathing. I felt like I could—" She burst into tears.

Father Rickie handed her a clean white handkerchief. "Could what?"

Through her miserable tears she said, "Like I could hear his heart beating, Father."

"When was this, my dear?"

"Ten years ago, Father."

"It was painful for you."

"It is now, Father. But then I thought it was what I wanted. I wanted to get rid of my inhibitions."

"And did you?"

She came up for air and worriedly glanced around the church. "He doesn't believe in marriage." Her chest hurt from the tears; she thought about Sharla, that Mona Lisa smile, what Sharla had concealed from Eddie. She wanted to say, *Tell* him what you want.

"Did you consider marriage?"

"I thought it might be a reasonable outcome, Father."

"That's what you think—"

"—when you're young. I know."

The rumors and temptations of people had not fully settled in Father Rickie's bones the way they had in hers. She saw through Eddie's exaggerated bonhomie. She understood Waverly's loneliness. And her mother drinking cold duck on the anniversary of her marriage to Jenny's father. In spite of everything, she did that. All that Jenny understood—what she had learned from all those secrets—was a gift from God, and that was one reason she had come to confession. They had something in common. She might know more than Father Rickie. Had he ever taken advantage of a girl? Had he ever reached down there without even a preliminary kiss? Had he ever ignored the girl after?

Eddie Fox had come up behind her while she admired the obsidian. It was a late summer evening, during the last heat wave of the year, right after classes had begun; the marching band practiced in a field not far away, tubas nickering. The canvas blinds were down. He complimented her body and no one had ever done that before—your hair, your hips, I watch you all the time, what is it with you? Look what you do to me, he said. She was twenty-two and still a virgin, still innocent of what it might mean not to be a virgin. She wasn't smart that way, but she knew it. Other girls were focused on getting the kind of attention that would result in hearts, flowers, rings, lace, wedding almonds, trips to the resort in French Lick. The whole kit-and-kaboodle, her mother called it. What they'd lost when her father left.

Jenny had a defect: a scar above her lip. When she was three years old, she had whirled dizzily in the living room, lost her balance, and struck the coffee table corner. Her father and mother, together, had whisked her to the emergency room at St. E's, where an old doctor with whiskey-breath did a sloppy job sewing her up. Every night she rubbed a cream used by women with stretch marks on the scar, willing it to go away. But it was still there, leathery, prickled, the size of a baby butter bean. He had not kissed her because of the scar, she felt sure.

Father Rickie was more interested in her admission of not going to Mass since she was thirteen. "Come tomorrow at seven-thirty," he said. "On Ash Wednesday, get your ashes before you go to work." For penance he told her to say five Hail Marys now and to come to daily Mass for a week.

The church had emptied out. She went up to the first pew and knelt down. Were the other priests waiting somewhere for Father Rickie? And what was his life like, after hearing confessions? Father Rickie went up to the altar and blew out the candles, cupping each flame with his hands. There was a humble shape to his back, a self-denigration he had adopted, even though he was young and good-looking. She would look forward to receiving Communion from him and doing her penance.

The altar and the sanctuary seemed to recede, lit only by a bank of lights in the rear of the church. When Father Rickie passed by, she reached out and returned his handkerchief.

"I'll wait in the back," he said. "I need to lock the doors. We keep the doors locked."

Jenny said the prayers—she could remember the words. But even as she prayed, the memory of Eddie, what she hadn't told Father Rickie, washed over her. How he had undressed her and she had not been ashamed. How sweaty they had been. How she had taken homemade cookies to him the next day. And the morning after that, a red lily, the only one in the crowded daylily bed on the alley behind the garage. All the others were Stella D'Ors that lit up the alley when sun struck there. She thought that surely if he appreciated the fossilized ferns in coal and the pink in granite, he would love the red lily. It was brick-red, with moist tough petals and an intricate interior. She had cut it down with a steak knife and wrapped its stem in a wet paper towel. In the geology lab, he had acted put out by her request for a vessel to put the red lily in. He had said he had a meeting. There had only been that one time when he praised her body and asked her to lie down with him on the army surplus blanket he kept in the lab cupboard, even though he visited her office every week and ate the miniature candy bars she kept on her desk.

She had been drunk on Eddie for years. That's what the tears are about, Father Rickie, she wanted to say. Almost the end of grief. A broken spell.

She stood up and genuflected in the aisle. Genuflecting, she recalled her First Communion. It was her father who had outfitted her. The rented veil. The white flats with the smooth soles. She had not thought of that since then, her father picking out the flats at the discount shoe store. He had come back for her First Communion, and he let her think it was from Ohio. Years later, she saw him from afar at the county fair with his new children, a boy and a girl. They were about to get on the Tilt-a-Whirl.

Father Rickie waited at the back near the stone baptismal font. He walked her to the door and said, "See you tomorrow." He touched her shoulder.

Outside, on the church steps, she was not weary. A windless night, it had begun to snow. The church was another place to be. Father Rickie was someone to get to know. She listened to the cheerful staticky voices of the taxi drivers in the parking lot of the convenience store, talking to each other on their radios. All things seemed new, vibrant. She could see her own house, the Christmas lights behind the grimy window. She might tell her mother about going to confession, or she might not. Her mother would have an opinion. She would never keep out of things or say, "That's up to you." Waverly's upstairs apartment glowed with TV light.

A half-block away there was a tavern with a sign in the window: HAND-SPANKED BURGERS. Two people were ducking into the tavern—like a somber painting, small-town life in winter—and she recognized them at once: Sharla and His Honor. Sharla wore a second-hand fur wrap and His Honor removed his fedora and opened the door for her. It was not a place you expected to see him. He probably thought it was ironic, taking Sharla there. He had explained irony to her. Professors went to the restaurants downtown near the courthouse, where you needed to know how to smell the cork when they brought the wine to your table.

What had felt momentarily sweet fermented. But it was a fix you could get, going to confession, like Eddie's city fix when he went to Chicago. She had a mean streak and at that moment she was grateful for it. She might uproot Waverly's herbs on the kitchen sill. She might hide her mother's menthols. A mean streak would give her something to talk about with Father Rickie, easier to confess than lust or greed. And she could predict that her mother would envy Father Rickie. She would dearly love to hear the stories, but Jenny would keep them from her. The future was all laid out. Jenny would be stuck with Sharla forever. She could see it in the way he opened the door for her. They would manage his affairs, make his travel arrangements to the theory conferences. Sharla might have his babies. She would not hurt the babies, but she would have to find a way to get back at her. Their lives would be linked by more than Sharla would ever know. Within a few days of each other, they had learned that what you want changes, and those who say never shouldn't.

SUN DAMAGE

JACK RANSOM DIED on the road.

That was to be expected. The day before Memorial Day, in Bloomington, he went into a coffee shop with another salesman. They ordered pecan pie and ice cream. Jack said he wasn't feeling well and went outside and sat down on the limestone steps and died. A heart attack.

Meg found out from her brother Vinnie who called her at Chico's in Santa Fe, right in the middle of the big summer sale. She'd tucked the phone between her shoulder and chin and kept on folding pale linen garments.

"Meg, please come. Help me round up Mother," he'd said. Among other things. Specifics about the funeral.

Meg was thirteen years older and she'd left home to live with Aunt Georgia when Vinnie was only three. Vinnie and Meg hardly knew each other. Their father had died and their mother needed rounding up. As though she were feral.

Meg wore dark glasses on the plane. She had not cried yet and expected to at any moment. She expected her eyes eventually to be puffy and tender to the touch. But the tears stalled. Vinnie had mentioned Terre Haute when Meg asked where he thought their mother—Hannah—might be. Terre Haute or the iris farm in Brookston with Jelly Cooke, her friend since high school. Hannah sometimes went out to Brookston for weeks on end and stayed with Jelly, her hands in the dirt during the day, helping out. At night, Vinnie said, she and Jelly went carousing. Meg was sure that was the word he used. That meant cards, no doubt. Hearts. A little gambling. A little gin. They probably dressed up in their clothes from God knows when— dresses from the fifties, with maddening pintucks, tough to iron.

If she were in Terre Haute she'd be harder to find. If people heard you'd come from there they'd say, "How long did it take you to get the smell out of your clothes?" Meg had seen Hannah's feelings hurt by such remarks. It was a smell both organic and industrial, putrid, persistent, uniform in its delivery. No one in the Wabash Valley was spared. Hannah was born there and had grown up in town, with plenty of silverware and china and linens. Her father owned a watch and clock shop and half the city block on which he lived. Everyone thought Hannah and her brother Dennis would fare even better in the world than their parents, but they hadn't. Hannah married Jack and moved to Tippecanoe County early on and Meg's Uncle Dennis followed. Before he retired, Dennis had been a mechanic at a meat packing plant. He had a little plot of land nearby, close to the slatternly village of Webber, and on that plot of land he grew a truck garden and sold strawberries and cucumbers and watermelons on muggy summer nights at a stand beside the road. He did not have a wife. Though later Meg had heard that he married a woman who kept bees. The wife had died young. In her fifties.

All of that happened while Meg was moving. She moved for twenty years. She followed Neil Diamond on tour for a year, obsessed with him. She could certainly see now what a brainless period that was. She worked in a logging camp in the North Cascades. She waited tables in Santa Cruz. She'd thought of herself as unencumbered, spontaneous. She'd changed her first name twice, to Heather and then to Laverna, Roman goddess of thieves, wanting first to be earthy, then neo-pagan. Though now she liked the sound of Meg. Margaret Mae Ransom. In business it helped to have a solid name. Her family had always been business people and she'd come to it late, but she loved it. During that time of moving around, she'd lived in apartments and houses with other women and sometimes she would have a man, sometimes two men, she'd be seeing and sleeping with. In those days, if she had a date, a night's worth of tips, a new dress or haircut, she was happy. It had not taken much. And the stories she heard about Uncle Dennis, and yes, even the stories she heard about her mother and father, from Vinnie and from letters Hannah wrote, those seemed like only stories, events in lives unconnected to her.

When Aunt Georgia died and left Meg a very, very small fortune—that was the way she always told the story—she moved to Santa Fe and invested in Chico's. She was settled. She lived alone. Her life was about order now. Getting up at six o'clock to meditate. Making sure the books were meticulously kept. Friends you could count on for a walk or a dinner. She rarely drank. She did not own a television. That sort of life. Her vices, if you could call them that, were clothes and an abiding interest in sex. She'd grown up Catholic and still went to Mass on Christmas Eve. But she and the Pope did not see eye to eye on birth control.

Jack had seldom written. Once in a while, after Hannah and he were no longer living together, he'd send Meg a blank card, a generic lace-and-roses card with a short message—*Happy Birthday, Baby,* or *Treat yourself*—and he'd send a check for twenty-five dollars or a fifty dollar bill. Meg always let Jack know where she was and she always let Hannah know where she was. That was the best she could do.

She'd never been a good daughter.

"What'd you say?" The woman next to her on the plane was speaking, a sinewy woman with opulent gray hair.

Meg said, "I beg your pardon?" She realized she must've spoken out loud.

"I thought you were speaking to me," the woman said. "Oh, look—"

Meg turned to the window.

"—we're almost down!"

There was Indy: neat, flat, easy. She picked out Speedway, a place she'd never been. And the White River, where she'd spent many an evening parked in this one's car or that. Panting. Giving an inch. The inch Hannah always warned her against.

She sighed at the thought of all she had to traverse: renting a car, the hour on the interstate, then the back roads and one-lane bridges. How much do you owe your blood relatives? This was a question that had burrowed into her like a taproot all day.

The woman in the next seat plucked a lipstick from her bag and applied it without a mirror. Lipstick as violet as vetch. Then she got out a pack of cigarettes and held it in one brown paw, done with Meg, done with the flight, eager for a smoke.

And Meg thought, Here we go. With a reluctant heart.

Vinnie let her into the house on Bicycle Bridge Road six miles out of Delphi. He still lived there, he and Jack. She had not seen Vinnie since he'd come to Santa Fe three years before. He was handsome, animated in a boyish way, with grins that would slip out as though he were shy. He wore baggy chinos and polo shirts in candy colors. He smelled the way young men smelled—like new clothes and some woodsy soap they used.

"It's kind of hard being here alone," he said. "I'm glad you're here."

He fed her couscous and broccoli and peppered feta cheese, the whole mound in a pasta dish, drizzled with olive oil. He gave her white wine to drink in a glass Meg knew belonged to Hannah. A wine glass etched with sunflowers. She drank the wine gratefully; what would it hurt? Their father had died and a glass of wine seemed ritualistic, a sign that life went on, a token of honor. Rain began to fall. Hard, necessary rain for the end of May. Clouds out the kitchen window bunched up, malevolent, bruisers. The wisteria tossed in the wind, its tendrils flying like a dancer's hair. They talked while the lights flickered. Jack had not been ill, far from it. He'd been talking about retiring. He'd been talking about moving to Naples, Florida. For the beach. "He'd gotten into a beach fantasy," Vinnie said. Vinnie had been looking forward to remodeling the house when Jack moved to Florida. Skylights. A second bathroom. A wood-fired hot tub under the sycamore tree. Modernization. A house built for a young man's pleasure. Vinnie worked for a contractor who built one-of-a-kind custom homes and he knew what to do with the weak floor joists and the old chimney and the worn-out plumbing and the austere kitchen with its aluminum cupboards.

Meg said, "We're all more prosperous now, aren't we?"

Vinnie folded his arms and began to cry. The thunder was so loud, Meg didn't notice at first. She'd bent to undo her sandals.

When she looked up, Vinnie's face was squeezed into grief. Meg felt a push—do something, comfort him. But she felt stuck to her chair. They had been close on occasion—they'd hugged goodbye, hello, and two-stepped self-consciously in a crowd when he'd visited. But she had not held him, for comfort, since he'd cut the ball of his foot on a sharp rock. There had been stitches at the emergency room. And Meg, fifteen, had rocked him to sleep after. Some Sarah Vaughn on the hi-fi.

She touched his arm.

Vinnie took a handkerchief—a folded, tidy square—out of his back pocket and pressed it against his cheeks. "I'm okay," he said.

Meg nodded. "Okay."

Thunder rolled away from them. Meg stood at the kitchen window over the sink. All plants—maple leaves, old lilacs, mock orange, grasses—shimmered in the wind and rain gloss. The green was deep. In Santa Fe you could forget that such green existed.

The phone rang. Vinnie ran a hand through his hair and answered it.

"Dennis," he said. "She's here. Yeah. We just ate. I'll put her on."

Meg shook her head, No, no. But it was too late. The beige receiver was in her hand, against her ear, and Uncle Dennis was saying, "How's tricks? Sorry you had to come back for this. Helluva thing."

"Uncle Dennis. How are you?"

He said, "I jog to keep my ticker tickin'. I'm almost seventy-three. Did you know that? And I've got a girlfriend—she's nearly eighty-four. She can dance like you wouldn't believe. We go to all the dances."

"That's good," Meg said. She pointed to her wine glass and Vinnie passed it to her. "We'll see you at the funeral home, I guess."

"I called to tell you where Hannah's at."

"Where is she?"

"Someone saw her at the Legion last night. Dressed fit to kill. She's a clothes horse still. Like you. So I've heard." He lowered his voice. "She's got something going with Lee at the hardware on the 52 bypass."

"I thought you were going to tell me where she is right now."

"I'm getting to that." He chuckled, an old-mannish accompaniment to gossip. Meg realized that gossip had been mostly weeded out of her life. This kind of gossip made you feel like dirt whether you were the giver or receiver.

Meg shoved the phone at Vinnie, her hand over the receiver. "I can't talk to him," she said. "I just can't. Just yet."

And when he hung up Meg said, "You're too good for this place, Vinnie."

Meg remembered a prowler, a season of fear, when she tried to piece together how Jack and Hannah had separated. This is what Vinnie wanted to hear about in her rental car, driving over to Battle Ground where Hannah had last been seen at RC's, a steakhouse.

"I think it started with that prowler. I was twelve or thirteen."

She'd been doing something she shouldn't have been—primping—when her mother came to her bedroom door and said, "I think there's a prowler outside." Then Hannah had shut off the overhead light in Meg's bedroom. It was nearly eight o'clock on a November night. The nearest neighbor was a quarter mile away. Vinnie was in his crib sound asleep. Jack Ransom was as usual somewhere in central Illinois or Indiana, though by that time of night, Meg imagined, he was standing at a bar. Sometimes while Hannah was in the bathroom, Meg would sneakily read the letters he'd written to her mother. *I believe I'll head down to the hotel bar for a nightcap, Sweetie pie.* She liked the words he used: nightcap, sweetie pie, severe weather, profit, long-range, Democrats. Her mother would never say sweetie pie.

"What should we do?" Meg whispered. She set down her mascara in its little red box, without a sound, as if the prowler could be disturbed by the slightest noise. Mascara seemed trivial then, though when the nuns warned all the seventh grade girls against primping, mascara took on the properties of magic, tool of sinners.

Wind like an old bed sheet wrapped around the house.

She had never before that moment thought that her mother

could be afraid in their own home. She thought of Hannah as pretty, bossy, and fearless. The summer before she had killed a black snake they had found in the bathtub, chopped him in two with a hoe.

"Come into the kitchen," Hannah whispered. She wore a chintz kimono and yellow scuffs and her face had been scrubbed pink.

Soundlessly they crept through the dining room; every room was dark; Meg was keenly aware that all of the windows but hers had no curtains. Her breastbone felt pummeled by her heart. Light, we need plenty of light in this old house. Hannah had taken down the curtains the summer before and never put them up again. Meg insisted upon privacy—brown paper blinds, and over those, opaque vinyl drapes from the Woolworth. What you could see outside the other windows of the house, the curtainless windows, what the eye chose to settle on, depended on the season: waves of snow, gray or gleaming; blooming redbud trees; black-eyed Susans branching taller and taller; or a maple with turning leaves. Or the dark, country dark, night like a dark broth.

Meg sat down at the kitchen table. She could smell fried potatoes. And scouring powder. Hannah went to the back door and checked the lock, snapping it open and closed. She carried the black telephone from its niche in the wall to the table; the cord just barely reached. She dialed the sheriff. It was busy.

They sat there for a quarter hour or more. Silence outside pressed against them and they pressed back, whispering of inconsequential things, shoes polished or not, a hole in one of the baby's mittens, the way Meg's pajamas hit her at the shin. An inordinate amount of time and energy went to the organizing of, the maintaining of, clothing. Hannah was a great proponent of mending. The other girls felt sorry for Meg because she only had one pair of shoes for school and one pair for Sunday Mass. Saddle oxfords and cream-colored flats. But she had lipsticks galore, greasy ones, handed down from a second cousin in Indianapolis. The same cousin stored her old prom gowns in a cedar closet, gowns Meg hoped to wear someday: velveteen and nylon net, rhinestones and bows.

Meg's teeth chattered. Wavelets of heat slipped through the radiator from the coal furnace in the basement. Hannah dialed up the sheriff's office every few minutes. The line was always busy.

"Times like this," Hannah said, "you need a man around the house."

Stories of men escaping from prison edged into Meg's mind. Stories of demented fellows who'd never been taught the Golden Rule.

"What would a man do?" Meg said.

"He'd open the door and pitch a fit. He'd have a gun, no doubt."

"Like Uncle Dennis."

Hannah made a vinegarish face; Meg could tell that in the dark.

"Don't hold your breath," Hannah said.

Truck headlights like luminous ropes swung into the driveway. A man was heard whistling—*I'm walkin' the floor over you*—and a truck door slammed.

Hannah went to the window and stood on tiptoe, peering out. "It's him," she said, irritated. Meg let out a big sigh. They heard Uncle Dennis crunching over the snow toward the house.

Hannah let him in and the cold came in with him. He was dressed in a plaid wool coat, boots with thick lug soles, and a hat trimmed in fox fur; Meg had a hard time telling his dishwater-blond hair and moustache from the fur.

Uncle Dennis said, "There's a peeping tom about. I came to check on you."

"You needn't've," Hannah said. "We're locked up tight and fine."

When Jack Ransom came home for Thanksgiving he installed a floodlight over the back door.

Everyone had rules and Meg Ransom learned them quickly, rather than risk getting a slap or the switch. When she'd grown up and left the house on Bicycle Bridge Road, Meg thought her mother's rules quite odd. But you don't know that when you're young; you imagine everyone lives as you do. Finding out that they don't is one of the best or worst discoveries of childhood. Hannah Ransom did not allow Meg to stare out the windows during lightning storms. She did not allow her to walk near people operating gasoline or electric lawn mowers. She did not allow her to watch television.

And she did not allow her to cross the railroad tracks into the lanes of Webber, a batch of leaning shotgun houses encircled by a muddy creek, the railroad tracks, and a sea of soybeans.

The houses were painted Easter egg colors and trash drifted in the plain dirt yards among the autos up on cinder blocks and the broken iceboxes. There was reputedly what polite people called a sporting house in Webber's inner region, beyond the prying eyes.

Jack Ransom sold sewing and yard goods gadgetry to fabric shops. He drove a black Studebaker that was nearly always coated with brown mud or dust or a film of road salt. The backseat was a jumble of yardsticks and pincushions shaped like tomatoes and wooden embroidery hoops and measuring meters, black boxes you could attach to a table for measuring out yard goods. His suit was brown worsted wool and too tight across his hips; he was heavier than when he'd bought it in 1955, and he could no longer button the jacket. But his shirts were nice. He had seven white ones and when he came home, every two weeks, Hannah washed them and starched the cuffs and collars and plackets. She ironed and hung the shirts on individual hangers in a canvas garment bag. He'd make the shirts last until he came home again.

Hannah had married Jack when she was twenty-three, against her parents' wishes, right after she'd come home from Wright-Patterson where she'd been a WAC until 1946. Her mother and father had not approved of her war effort. They had hoped she'd still be a girl when the war was over, that she would move back in with them and wait for the right man to come along. But Hannah met Jack on the train that brought her back home from Dayton. Once Meg had said, "Why did you marry Dad, anyway, Mama?" And Hannah had said, "He blessed me whenever I sneezed." Now Meg understands Hannah's need to deflect the question.

By the time Vinnie was born Hannah had given up for herself, but she still thought her children might have a better life. She could imagine it. On a knick-knack shelf above the kitchen stove Hannah kept a ceramic vase she had made in high school. It was glazed midnight blue and had been built using the coil method. The vase was not handsome, Meg knew that for sure, but her mother could look at it and imagine a flute concerto. The ugly blue vase was Hannah's idol, Meg thought, and her reason for sending her to Catholic school and saving to buy a second-hand upright piano and not allowing her to play in Webber, where the children bathed only once a week. And smoked. And performed other unspoken secret acts that made their eyes glitter in shame and slyness on the school bus.

If there was gossip, Hannah attributed it to the Pentecostals whose house was situated in the middle of a cornfield. She was sure they kept a close watch on her—a married woman left alone, always suspect. Meg rode the school bus with their boy Glenn, a thin, scowling junior who attended the consolidated high school and defiantly slicked his blond hair into a duck's tail. He worked for Uncle Dennis, tilling and planting and picking. From her own bedroom Meg could see the light in what she thought was his bedroom, a yellow pinprick in the winter night. On the bus she smiled at him suggestively. Later, alone, she'd wonder what made her do it. But she wanted him. Hannah would say, "Stay away from him. He's not what he's cracked up to be."

Meg said to Vinnie, "Whatever happened to him—you know, Glenn—who lived down the road?" Her mouth had dried out from the wine. They crossed a bridge over the muddy Wabash.

Vinnie said, "He's around. He went in the war—Vietnam— and he came back and married a woman who'd never cut her hair. Her Dad gave them a piece of land. I think they grow cut flowers and tomatoes and sell 'em at the farmer's market."

"That can't be all they do."

"He works at Subaru, I think."

"How do you know?"

"Osmosis," Vinnie said.

Dusk had always signaled a calm solitude, a peace to Meg and Hannah, all chores done. But after the prowler incident, because his identity had never been ferreted out or revealed, they were watchful, on-edge. Rex Pratt delivered diapers at just that time of day after the Christmas holidays. He was youngish, tall, tall enough that he hunched over from the neck down like an ungainly bird when he spoke with women and children—and his hair curled on his neck, haircuts forgotten. He had the habit of petting his moustache with his thumb and forefinger, as if to make certain he still had it. He carried a key ring of five-inch long safety pins, and twice a week he came to truck away the soiled diapers and bring bundles of snowy clean ones. He took his time with everything, lingering, Hannah said, because he liked the air in the country. On his ring finger he wore a flat gold band. At first they would stand in the darkening kitchen, Rex beside the pie safe, leaning on the door frame, as if to say, I'm really on my way out, and Hannah near the sink with a dishrag in her hand, the big oak table between them. She did not turn on the light. They would talk for ten or fifteen minutes. He had a kind voice.

As the days lengthened, so too their conversations.

In March, while washing baby bottles at the sink, Hannah said to Meg, "When the diaper man comes, stay in the room."

"What for?" Meg said.

"Just read or whatnot," Hannah said, "but stay in the kitchen."

Meg sighed.

"Young lady—"

"Oh, all right," Meg said, gritting her teeth. And she began the habit of reading her library books, or pretending to, while Rex Pratt and Hannah talked.

Rex would sit at the table, with his chair turned sideways and his hands on his knees. A formal pose. Hannah continued to stand, though before he arrived she would brush her hair—a quick, jabbing stroke or two—and she would put on a gold cross pendant that slipped perilously between her breasts. You would never notice Hannah's modest neckline of her modest blouse if not for that cross. They would drink wine from Hannah's good glasses.

Meg's interest in their talk ebbed and flowed, though she always feigned indifference. Once Hannah showed Rex a photograph of Uncle Dennis in his war uniform. His cheeks had been tinted in an unnatural way. Handsome. Though some might say handsome is as handsome does. He was a prince. When I was a girl. When I was a girl, Meg would repeat to herself. She tried to picture Hannah as a girl. A town girl in white cotton gloves, a proper girl who did not pit herself against her mother—that's how Meg imagined her.

She read and daydreamed while Hannah talked with Rex, only vaguely recognizing the steps they took, confessing bit by bit. They were getting down to something, excavating delicately.

On the first official day of spring—a day windy and cool, with the sun still wintry and pale overhead—Meg held her books on the school bus and stared out the window at the greening countryside. Glenn sat down beside her, in a tattersall shirt and windbreaker. He wore English Leather. They sold it at the Woolworth in Lafayette. English Leather seemed made to attract girls. What did his Pentecostal mother think of that?

"I'm workin' for your uncle now," he said.

"It's planting time?" She thought that she sounded like her mother.

"Not quite. We're organizing. Diggin' in some manure."

She did not think he would say manure to Uncle Dennis. It would be shit plain and simple and she took that as a sign of respect. Everyone said it was important for a boy to respect you. He stared straight ahead.

"I work there after school," he said. "Your Uncle ain't home until dark."

These words rooted in Meg.

Two days later she said to Hannah, "I'm going for a bike ride."

"In this weather?"

"It's not so bad."

The blustery sky was softly gray like a mourning dove's chest.

"The diaper man's coming," Hannah said.

Meg waited.

"Don't go today, Meg," Hannah said. "I'm baking. I need you here to tend to Vinnie."

Meg sighed. "When can I go?"

"When the weather improves there'll be plenty of time for that."

"I'm not a baby."

Hannah silenced her with a look. There was and always had been a rule about backtalk. You did as you were told. The body remembers pain. When Hannah gave Meg that look, Meg felt a tingling across her face—ghost of Hannah's palm.

She picked up her homework, a list of spelling words to memorize: gender, genre, gelatinous. She sat beside the telephone niche and wrote the words over and over again, using a clipboard to keep her paper straight. And Glenn. Glenn. Glenn. She wrote that while Hannah and Rex talked. My brother, too. All dressed up with no place to go. Torment. Foxtrots. No, waltzes. There were times like that. Kelly was my high school sweetheart. I never—

"Who's Kelly?" Meg once said.

"Kelly's his wife," Hannah said. "His little wife."

When Jack Ransom next came home, Hannah said, "I want to have a Sunday dinner, with company."

"What company?" Jack said. He sat at the kitchen table in his undershirt. A ledger was open before him, a glass of whiskey near his hand. It was a warm day. Hannah had opened all the windows and breezes blew throughout the house.

"A couple. Rex and Kelly. They're driving out looking for a place in the country. We rarely get to do that, Jack. You being gone."

"All right," Jack Ransom said. "I'll have to leave in the evening. You mean mid-day? After Mass?"

"After Mass. Yes."

And so it was arranged. Rex and Kelly would come to Sunday dinner the next time Jack was home. Hannah went about her preparations. The tile floors were swept and scrubbed, the corners scraped with an old paring knife. Rugs were hung on the clothesline and beaten. The furniture was given a coat of beeswax and oil that smelled like oranges. Linens were mended. The house felt like Christmas. And just as at Christmas, Meg was set free by her mother's preoccupations. Hannah flew about the house, her dark hair pulled into a ponytail, slamming drawers, vacuuming, straightening. The hi-fi would be on: Mendelssohn, music sweet enough to make Hannah cry.

On the Wednesday before, after school, Meg said, "Just a short ride, that's all I want."

Hannah looked at the clock. She said, "Rex'll be here soon. You come back, hear? Come back in half an hour."

"Yes, Mother," Meg said, feeling her heart move like a hand opening.

She wheeled her blue bicycle down to the end of the driveway. It was still cool and a wind blew up from the river. But she did not want to go back for a sweater. She wore blue jeans rolled up at the bottom and bobby sox and saddle oxfords and a white blouse. She pulled a tiny round mirror and a lipstick from her pocket. She stood beside her bicycle and ducked close to the mirror and painted on the lipstick called Sugar 'n Spice. The thought of going to confession entered her mind, but she pushed that thought away. She hid the mirror and lipstick in among a clump of daffodils and took off flying at breakneck speed down the road. Goosebumps rose all over her body.

At her uncle's trailer she let her bicycle fall to the ground. Big clouds brewed above. Glenn's bicycle lay outside the greenhouse. She went to the door. He knelt beside a flat of strawberry seedlings. His fingers were muddy.

"Meg," he said, surprised to see her. "What you up to?"

She stepped into the greenhouse and it was warm inside and humid and smelled of dirt and foliage. The opaque glass walls made her feel protected.

"Is my Uncle here?"

"He don't come until dark. I told you."

Doesn't. She said, "Can I watch you?"

He grinned. "You can help me."

He showed her how to prick out a seedling and plant it into a peat pot, how to hold it from the bottom leaves that come first from the seed. "Try to not ever touch the roots," he said. "They're fragile." He pronounced it fra-gile. Meg hadn't known he could be so gentle.

After a while they stood side by side at the counter. Glenn said, "Why do you have that stuff on your mouth?"

"I like it," she said.

"You look better without it."

She wiped her mouth with her forearm and a rosy smear came off. He turned her around and kissed her, leaving muddy fingerprints on her blouse. She kissed him back; it surprised her that she knew how.

"Here," he said, turning on the hose at his feet, "let's wash our hands."

She did as he said. She wiped her cold wet hands on her blue jeans.

"I know a place we can go. He won't be back for a bit." He

lifted a folded tarp from a shelf and took her hand.

Outside the sky darkened with the storm. Wind blew hard and velvety topsoil was swept away from the newly tilled field. The kerosene lamps of Webber were being lit. She had never been so close to Webber at dark. She wondered what the people there were doing. He led her to the steps of the trailer on a knoll and the steps to the porch were steep. It was underneath the steps he was leading her, through a small opening in the canes of the rambling rose.

He went under and spread the tarp on the ground while she shivered and watched the sky. He said, "Hurry up. It's okay."

Meg crawled under the porch. A rose thorn scratched her arm. Under the porch was dim, cobwebby. He kissed her scratch, to make it better, he said. He pinned her down and lay on top of her. A rock or walnut shell poked into her back. He kissed her face, stickily. He licked her face. Thunder clapped; it sounded as if it came from the river. He pressed the part she had always wondered about against her. He took it out and said, please, please—

She touched him. It felt like being in a science experiment. Her fingers icy. That part of him warm. She wondered, Did all of his body heat come from there? She said, "I'm not fourteen yet."

"I won't hurt you," he said.

"My mother's wondering where I am."

He said, "Your mother's got her delivery man."

She jerked her hand away. "What're you talking about?"

He leaned back on his elbows, glanced away arrogantly. "My ma says she don't miss a trick." He gripped her wrist. "Come on—"

"I've got to go home," she said, scrambling away from him. "Let me out."

She crawled out between the canes. Uncle Dennis pulled into the driveway. He laughed when he saw her. He got out of the truck and clomped up to the porch. Glenn came out from under the porch; he hung his head sheepishly and busied himself with folding the tarp. A wave of hail rattled down. The lamp in the greenhouse was on—yellow against the skillet-black night. The trees, the trailer, the drive, the clouds and sky—all were blackening with the storm. Tree limbs whipped around. Rain began to fall in cold needles.

"What a sight you are," Uncle Dennis said. He shoved Glenn between his shoulder blades. "Git home," he growled. "I'll deal with you tomorrow."

Glenn slid the tarp onto the porch and pushed his bike down to the road, his skin slick with the rain, his clothes soaked.

"Go inside," Uncle Dennis said. Though he told her what to do, Meg could sense that he was coaxing her. There was something in his voice he didn't quite have control over.

"I want to go home."

"Can't you see it's fixin' to storm bad? There's a tornado warning, girl."

Uncle Dennis held her hand and led her inside the trailer. His hand was big as a catcher's mitt, every fingernail outlined with grease. He turned on the electric heat and a lamp. He took a brown quart bottle of beer from the refrigerator. Sterling Beer. He sat down at the table and poured a glass and rolled a cigarette. But he didn't light it. He held it by each end and stared at the cigarette as if it could tell the future. In the tiny trailer kitchen, Meg wrapped her arms around herself, watching out the window. She shuddered. Her bicycle was out in the rain and she did not like that. She spied a stack of movie magazines.

"I saved those for you," Uncle Dennis said. Then, "Call your mother. She'll be worried sick."

Meg picked up the receiver and dialed. She spoke to Hannah haltingly. Hannah asked to speak to Uncle Dennis.

"I'll look after her," he said. "Now don't worry none. Storm's over, I'll bring her home." He met Meg's eyes. She looked away. "Hold your horses, Hannah."

He hung up. The trailer creaked in the wind. He said, "Cat got your tongue?"

She stared at his row of blooming African violets. He liked to plant things. He was a man with violets. This way of seeing him brought up buffeting, half-formed thoughts, embarrassed denials, tender urges. She had never thought of him as a man before. With her back to him she said, "Can I look at those magazines?"

"We better clean up first."

At the sink he took off his work shirt and scrubbed his hands and arms. His back was winter white and muscular. He said, "Why don't you clean up? In there." He nodded toward the bathroom. "I guarantee your mama'll treat you better if you clean up. I know her pretty good."

Meg went into the bathroom and shut the door. His shaving things were on a shelf above the basin, a silver razor, a brush, an Old Spice lather mug. She held her breath, thinking she did not want to be in her Uncle's bathroom or to smell his smells. But when she inhaled, there was no foreign odor. She washed her face and arms and combed her hair with his black pocket comb. Her face looked different. She was certain she was the only girl in seventh grade to have been kissed. To have touched a boy down there. It was all she had been warned against. She unbuttoned her blouse and tried to wash out the mud prints. Her cotton brassiere wrinkled where she did not fill it.

Uncle Dennis knocked on the door. She opened it brazenly.

"Next time you're all dressed up with no place to go," he said, "come visit your Uncle Dennis."

There was a hint of gratitude in his voice, an emotional pitch she'd never heard before. "Take me home," she said.

"After the storm," he said. He touched her shoulder. His fingers felt like sandpaper. Then he shut the door.

At home, Hannah beat her with a wooden spoon. The baby stood up in his playpen and screamed bloody murder. His diaper was falling down. Hannah chased Meg from room to room. Hannah's hair was loose and tangled. She squealed and Meg could see into her mouth, her big teeth stained with coffee. Hannah cried and swore with words Meg had never heard or read in books.

She brayed, "He'll never come back. You left me here, you left me. With *him*. And what were you doing? Don't you know he's not to be trusted? Don't you know that? I can't let you out of my sight." She paddled her with the wooden spoon, and when the wooden spoon broke, she slapped Meg's face, each cheek.

Meg sobbed underneath the oak table. Hannah sat down on a chair, her legs splayed wide, hanging her head. The kitchen light shined on her nose—an orange streak—where she'd hastily wiped on the wrong color face powder. She hissed, "Get away from me."

In her room, Meg slumped onto the bed, dirty as she was. She could be alone there with the dream of pleasure: please, please, the baby skin of it.

Secrets she knew how to keep. Some parts she'd keep from Vinnie. Memory serves us in ways that allow us to go on with a little dignity. She could stand to recall everything. But there was no sense telling everything. At some point what you told became only gossip on yourself, stirring up old trouble. And no good can come from that.

It was dark by the time Vinnie and Meg pulled into Battle Ground and turned down the pocked narrow road that ran along the railroad tracks. RC's parking lot was full. She parked across the road in a stand of fireweed. They sat in the car for a minute, steeling themselves.

"How come you didn't ask me all this before?"

Vinnie said, "Jack didn't want me to. Oh, he didn't come right out with it. But I got the drift."

Meg said, "How often do you see Hannah?"

"Pretty often."

"That's good, I guess," she said.

"I wish I could see you more often."

In a soft voice, Meg said, "Is that so?" Then, "I wonder how they fit so many people in there?"

"Let's check it out." Vinnie got out and opened her door. The rain had faded away and killer mosquitoes swarmed to their flesh, lighting, biting.

The ceiling was low in RC's, the room smoky blue. A jukebox played honky-tonk. Diners were crammed at little Formica tables spread with slabs of meat, bowls of slaw, glass pitchers of iced tea and beer. The walls were brown with the fumes of grilled steak, the accumulation of decades.

"That smell," Meg said, "makes me hungry."

"That's why we conquered the West," Vinnie said, coming close to her ear to speak, nearly pecking her ear. "Look. At the bar."

At the bar in the back of RC's perched Hannah, a wad of tissue in one fist. Her print dress seemed trendy, definitely too young for her, Meg determined. Not at all the way she had expected to find her. At that moment she spitefully realized, Of course, Hannah would have moved on fashion-wise, that's what Hannah did best. Meg was afraid she might say exactly what she was thinking. Not a good policy. Strangely, she remembered a friend telling her about his trip to New Zealand, how every day he would see people on the street with scars from sun cancer. No more ozone down there, he said. Hannah's hair had been shaped by an expert: a shiny black-from-a-bottle hood, stacked in the back. Her hair swung cheerily when she turned to them. She punched out her cigarette in the ashtray. She'd been crying.

"Jelly, Jelly," she squeaked. "Look who's here." And Hannah rushed toward them, nearly colliding with the waitress who held a tray aloft, her midriff bare and sloppy below a spangled bustier.

"Mother." Vinnie spoke first.

Hannah hugged Meg and Hannah smelled good, a capsule of well-groomed female scents in the middle of the stale beer and steak and grease. She reared back and stared into Meg's eyes. The hair on Meg's head prickled in memory of hurt. Music jarred them, a ballad ballooning from the jukebox, and the three of them managed to move haltingly to the bar where Jelly in her big woman's one-size T-shirt and tights, her voice rough, tried to greet them, tried and managed to express her complicity in their grief about Jack, without Meg understanding anything that was said. The music was too loud. Jelly pushed a big box of tissues toward Meg.

"I have to find the bathroom," Meg said to Hannah. Hannah pointed her in the right direction.

The bathroom was cramped. In there, no one had scraped the corners with a paring knife for a long time. Maybe never. A chrome condom machine hung on the wall across from the mirror. She washed her hands, combed her hair, put on hand lotion. The sun can kill you now. She thought about all the times she had lain in the sun without a care, the way the sun made her flesh iridescent brown so that she herself liked touching it, smoothing on lotion, so that a man might want to do the same. Long touches. Gin days.

Beaches without a worry. The glory of all that. She still thought of it as glory. Those were her twenties. Jack would never know the beach. She thought of him in his hotel rooms in all the strange towns. The scant bars of hard soap. The way you had to go out for the merest consolation, a cup of coffee or a newspaper. That's when she cried. Niggardly tears. Sweetie pie. He'd always called her sweetie pie. There was always so much he didn't know.

Outside, the lightning bugs lit up.

Vinnie and Meg and their mother stood outside RC's while the Amtrak train went by on its way to Chicago. It was the first time they'd stood on the same ground in a long time. Someone had died. Someone connected to them. A black waiter listed on the steps of a dining car, smoking a cigar. Meg slipped her arm through Vinnie's, squeezed his hand. Hannah said something, her mouth open, darker than the dark, but the train was grinding by. When the train had passed, Hannah gingerly leaned in close and said, "Don't be afraid of me, Meg."

Hannah had lived with Jack three more years after Rex was in their lives. She waited until her parents passed away and left her money. Money can change everything, not only the way you meet your obligations, but the very nature of those obligations. Meg had gone to Aunt Georgia's and Jack hired a housekeeper—a woman who needed a place to live—to come in and care for Vinnie. Hannah moved to town, first to Delphi, then to Lafayette, then to Terre Haute. She kept a post office box in Delphi, but Meg had not been sure where Hannah slept most nights. She swore she would never live in the country again. Living like that, taking the Greyhound from town to town, acquaintance to acquaintance, to make the money last, with the clothes she could fit into a big blue Samsonite suitcase—Meg did not know how she stood it. She thought that Hannah saw her life as though she were a character in some nineteenth century novel. Spending a fortnight here or there. Always with lemonade in tall glasses on a side porch. The orange daylilies in view. Wicker furniture. A game of hearts to lighten the load of a humid summer afternoon.

The morning after Hannah had beaten her with the wooden spoon, Glenn did not sit down beside her on the school bus. No one had said a word about the bruises on her arm. Not even Jack Ransom, who came home on Friday night. Hannah told him that the Sunday dinner had been cancelled. He suggested they invite Dennis. Dennis could bring his shotgun over and they could kill the possums in the ravine where they threw their trash.

At Sunday dinner Uncle Dennis sketched out his plans for the truck garden. Glenn, the Pentecostal boy, would work for him all summer. He trusted him, he said. He wanted to know if Meg would like to sell strawberries during the month of June. Glenn could show her all about it. I'm only a piece up the road, he said to Hannah, you can keep an eye on her.

Jack said, "That'll give the girl some business sense."

Hannah said, "I need her here."

Meg detected in her mother a relenting, tiredness, and she thought that eventually she would allow her to sell strawberries at the roadside stand. And Hannah would search Meg for signs of squalor every time she came home.

Jack Ransom and Uncle Dennis went out to the ravine to kill possums. It was nearly dark when they returned. Hannah was changing the baby's diaper. Meg sat at the treadle sewing machine, staring out the front window, ready to weep. Hannah had not spoken directly to her all the long weekend. What mysterious grief she and Rex Pratt had worked over those stolen winter afternoons. Hannah had not gone to communion that morning. But Meg had gone, morosely, a cloud of doom hanging over her. She had chewed the dry host, though girls at her school thought it more solicitous of Jesus to let it melt.

"Boo!" Uncle Dennis popped up into view, out on the porch. Her father was nowhere around.

She burst into tears.

"Don't cry, Sugar," Uncle Dennis said, through the window

glass. "I didn't mean to scare you that bad." His voice was muffled, an arabesque of seduction and danger and care. Beyond him a row of slim red tulips had closed for the night.

NO REFUNDS
IN CASE
OF INCLEMENT WEATHER

ELLEN WINTERS FELT CLUELESS about lovers and cars, but she needed one of each. Newsprint ink from the classified section rubbed off on her hands. Not the end of the world—she had cobwebby clay under her fingernails and a stain of rose madder on her fingertips.

Her mother—Postmistress of Battle Ground—slammed shut the till and jerked down the blind on her customer window. "Rumor has it," her mother said, "you can order up a car—whatever you want—at the credit union. Like takeout."

By that she meant: I don't want you out and about, shopping for a used car. Men sell used cars from their dim and oily garages. It's not safe.

Ellen batted the newspaper with the back of her hand. Out the window she spied pointillist birch leaves and a Springer spaniel she knew. Kids desperate to hang out somewhere, anywhere, lounged in front of the Pizza King. One girl did a toe-rocking thing with a skateboard and the board banged against the sidewalk. It was April, with daylight lasting until nearly seven. "I like the ads," she said. "Listen: 'Check this out! Ford 78. Thunderbird. 84K miles. One-owner. Garage-kept. $1999. OBO.'"

Her mother slipped out of running shoes and into kitten heels. She sashayed out to lower the flag; wind rattled the rigging against the flagpole.

Ellen had homework. When she remembers that day nearly nine years ago, she thinks of homework always nipping at her heels. Twenty-three years old, a super-super-senior (from stopping out and working at a halfway house for women of the street in Chicago), she wanted to graduate in December. She had projects due two weeks hence.

Her mother came back in, the flag all wadded up.

Ellen said, "I'm out of here."

"Where to?"

"The river."

Her mother dangled the Volvo key she kept on a separate key ring, a silver-dollar-size labyrinth. Labyrinths, Tarot cards, runes, I-Ching sticks: these were the accoutrements of her mother's spiritual journey. "You're meeting Gatling."

"I might be." Indeed, she was supposed to meet Gatling, a guy from a band called Blue Sugar. A guy too young for her, but she didn't see anyone else on the horizon. He was sweet the way puppies are sweet. He was what she could handle, after what had happened in Chicago. But he had no future, as her mother always felt obliged to point out.

Then: "Watch out for Tommy Mattingly."

Ellen swiped the key and pocketed it. "Give me a break."

Her mother squared back her shoulders, her breasts alert under a Lycra-enhanced sweater. In her fifties, she was good-looking, married for the fourth time, with no lack of men in her life. Ellen saw herself as opposite: short, freckled, a little pudgy, but compact, with out-of-control curly hair she restrained with kerchiefs and cloches. A frequenter of second-hand shops, she liked to mix-and-match odd prints and stripes, almost, not quite, a slap in the face to her stylish mother. She wore socks a grade-school girl would wear, printed with palm trees or snowmen.

Her mother lit up a Marlboro and blew smoke to the pressed-tin ceiling. "I know whereof I speak."

It wasn't a park yet, the day her mother warned her about Tommy Mattingly. Land for a state park had been set aside down by the Wabash River, but for the longest time there was nothing there but a caretaker's house with loose gutters, a tractor shed, fields of

prairie flowers cut with a wide swath—a trail that went nowhere—
and six Clydesdale horses. You could drive right up to the caretaker's place and park—Tommy Mattingly was the caretaker—and
take a walk. Not that many people did. They lived in a part of the
Midwest where you had to drive to get anywhere. Walkers were
suspect, associated with tree huggers and Unitarians.

Her mother didn't understand that there was no safer place
than empty fields, sky, wind, and the river beyond with anglers in
a johnboat. Ellen had come home from Chicago after two girls at-
tacked her in the parking lot of the halfway house. Whenever she
told the story she tried to keep it simple. A bitter-cold afternoon
in early December. They couldn't have been over thirteen. She was
leaning into the back seat of her boss's SUV, gathering up bottles of
water to give away on the street. Bottles of water and pamphlets for
the help they offered: STD tests, showers, hot meals, counseling.
Handing out water and pamphlets was her job, for the most part,
although occasionally she was allowed to do what her internship
prescribed: art therapy with the children. She would sit at a low
table and say whatever would keep them drawing and painting.
Good colors. Can you tell me about it?

The girls shoved her down, kicked her, and took her wallet.
She had grown at ease in the neighborhood, among the trash and
the sloe-eyed loitering men, the wary Polish crones with their
string bags, the snotty-nosed children; her reaction was near as-
tonishment. The doctor said one kidney was bruised. One hand
had been ground into the gravel. Antibiotics for the staph infec-
tion on her hand disturbed the good bacteria in her digestive tract
and what she called her nether regions. She quit the internship,
lost the deposit on her studio apartment, and went home to her
mother. And her mother thought she could protect her with rote
warnings about men.

Ellen waited by the tractor shed for Gatling, her boots sucking in
the mud, but he did not show. She did not feel undone by his absence. That made her think, I guess he's not the one. They hadn't

slept together yet. He was the sort of boy who said, in an affected manner, when things went his way, "Life's all peaches and tits, ain't it?" She knew it was affected—he'd been a straight A student at St. Pat's and at St. Pat's they taught them to diagram sentences and use proper grammar. On a bad day he said, "It's a royal bummer." He had little discernment beyond that. But his energy when he played his electric guitar made her laugh; he was goofy and fun. Oh, well.

Claire Lowry was the caretaker's girlfriend. That's all Ellen knew the first time they talked. Later she found out that Claire was a Classics professor at the university. In spite of those six months in the real world of Chicago, Ellen had a hard time imagining professors outside the classroom or the espresso shop where one or two might stop by late at night when students studied with their books sprawled across the tables. The professors never did more than wave to the students.

Ellen and Claire met walking on the trail that spring afternoon when almost all Ellen could think about was finding a car so she wouldn't have to borrow her mother's Volvo. She needed to break away. *Garage-kept* sounded virginal. *OBO* sounded hard up. Fog floated from the river. Claire Lowry had a blind dog named Flapjack, part Border collie, and the dog stopped to sniff at Ellen's boots. They were the only people for miles around. The nearest town was Battle Ground, five miles west, and Ellen sometimes thinks back to her naïveté—she assumed that no one would ever suspect that two women were falling in love or lust, whatever it was at first, down by the Wabash, wind damp in their faces. Claire was over forty. Ellen couldn't quite tell, but she seemed almost as old as her mother.

Ellen's mother—Vivian Winters—bore the last name of Ellen's father, even though she had been married three times after that. I'm on a roll, she would say, when talk among women turned to marriage. Husband #4 would find this funny—he was sort of a homegrown comic himself, always making fat jokes (which he wasn't) and loser jokes, which some might say he was, but Ellen didn't think so. He was a basement-inventor who held no patents. Vivian Winters never said she was on a roll in front of him. Some things you don't say to a man, Ellen learned early on. At great sacrifice, when Ellen was a baby, Vivian became a teacher—she went to classes at night and did her homework even later, with Letterman at a whisper on the television. She found a job teaching second grade, but husband #2 resented the dish tub full of worksheets she hauled home every night. She took the civil service test, became the postmistress at the Battle Ground post office, and never looked back.

Ellen loved her to pieces but she did not want to become her mother. To that end, she didn't smoke. She wore her short hair threaded with orange the color of roadwork signs (to go in the opposite direction of Vivian, who thought big blond hair was sexy), and she swore that she would not make commitments she couldn't keep. Her mother lived to please. She dealt in rumor, but not maliciously. She wore pointy shoes that showed off her legs. She could predict the Heisman winner and was a great fan of Peyton Manning. The sort of woman men liked.

After that first time talking with Claire on the trail, Ellen went back to her mother and said, "So what's the story with Tommy Mattingly?"

Her mother opened the cap on a jar in which she was brewing cranberry-orange vodka. She poured an inch of the ruby-toned vodka into a juice glass and took a sip before she spoke. She pursed her lips. "Needs more sugar," she said.

That's her slogan, her mantra, Ellen thought. *Needs more sugar.* Beyond the kitchen window, husband #4 rototilled a deep garden patch defined by railroad ties. He wore a newsboy's cap and did not look like a gardener. More like a bon vivant. The rototiller growled distantly, a sound Ellen associated with spring, school ending, all things new. A time to paint outdoors. Watercolors especially appealed to her—she could expect happy accidents. She wanted to spend the summer painting, but she needed a job. Something temporary that would not require new clothes or even an attitude adjustment.

Vivian cranked open the casement window beside the breakfast table. From a pack, she tapped out a cigarette and said, "You mind?"

"It's your house." After living alone in Chicago, it had felt ignoble to come back to her mother. #4 commented on her vegetarian diet. They giggled upstairs—she felt lonely when they did. Sometimes her mother put on dance music, Tommy Dorsey or Glenn Miller, and they danced and giggled in the kitchen. Their lives were all about domestic excess, too much wine and garlic. Finally Ellen bought earplugs—the kind you use for target practice.

Vivian lit up a cigarette and waved the smoke out the open window and told stories Ellen thought she had heard before, but always with half an ear. Tommy Mattingly was older than her mother and had never been on Ellen's radar. Vivian called him a ladies' man. At mixers in the high school gym, he had taught her to shimmy to songs like "Little Deuce Coupe." He had a car he had rebuilt—in the sixties—and the car was from before the last world war. He babied that car. Later, for a year or so, he lived with hippies in a tree house or a house built around trees. There had been wild parties. Hallucinogenic. Drunken. With people crashing in sleeping bags beside the remains of a campfire. Waking up with headaches to emotional ruin. Vivian said that Tommy Mattingly was still a ladies' man. He sniffed out available women and lorded his power over them, is what she said.

"And that would be?" Ellen said.

"Chemistry, kiddo. That man's power is all about chemistry."

The third time Claire and Ellen met on the trail, Claire invited her back to the caretaker's house. She showed her the Clydesdale horses, gargantuan, living right behind the house in a fenced lot they churned to mud with their big hooves. The caretaker's kitchen was in a country mess, with canning equipment stacked in one corner, avocado pits suspended by toothpicks in glasses of murky water on the windowsill, and cookbooks open on the table, the pages stained. Evidence of a man—Redwing boots by the door, filthy jeans in a pile near the washer—put Ellen on guard. He might walk in at any moment.

She wanted him to stay away. Ellen listed close to Claire while she stood on tiptoe and sorted through tea boxes in the cupboard until she came to ginger lemon. Claire set the box on the counter and said, "Do you—have you—ever—loved a woman?"

After that Tommy ceased to be anyone Ellen might care about, even in a rudimentary ethical way. Within a month, Ellen had moved into Claire's apartment in the converted armory. The apartments had high ceilings and windows overlooking a park where people played chess in summer. They became a couple. Claire rode her motor scooter for errands, walked to campus, and she gave Ellen the use of her car, a sky blue Rambler station wagon that had belonged to her grandmother. At first, they did not touch in public, but gradually they did, they couldn't help themselves, and the next year, when the university extended benefits to same-sex partners, they had a coming out party to announce a forthcoming commitment ceremony.

Claire's breakup with Tommy had been congenial; he kept Flapjack, who loved to roam the state park property. Tommy came to the party with his new girlfriend, another professor who had devoted herself to her scholarly career—she studied companion animal behavior—until she found herself still alone at age forty-one, wanting more.

Claire knew what women wanted. The first time they made love, Ellen had three orgasms in quick succession. Nothing like that had ever happened to her. She was grateful. Claire had not had children; her body was like a girl's, with a long, lean stomach. She unpinned her wavy pale hair when they went to bed. She looked like a woman in a painting—"The Lady of Shalott."

The first year they spent so much time in bed that Ellen's graduation became a footnote. She took a job in an art supply store. Her boss said that eventually she could give watercolor lessons. They bought a house and considered having a baby, but decided in a few wine-marinated conversations that their freedom was more important. They finished each other's sentences. On Sunday afternoons, in the bittersweet hours from three to seven, they held an open house for friends and students and neighbors. Liquor flowed, cheesecakes were consumed, congenial arguments ensued, books were loaned, romances plotted—it was a heady, lovely time, those years.

That was one version. But it had been rockier than they cared to remember. Vivian had flipped out. In Claire's company she was polite. She had invited Claire to dinner, just as you would a man your daughter dated. She prepared her best dishes, pork loin and chocolate mousse. She lit the candles in the Italian candlesticks. But when Claire left the house, and she and Ellen were cleaning up, and #4 was in the basement, Vivian started in.

Later, Claire would say, "We don't have to do this. If it's coming between you and your family."

And Ellen said, "It's not. I wasn't that close to them anyway." When Ellen was alone with her mother, Vivian badgered her. Ellen avoided her much of the time, hoarding any unfinished business.

The house Ellen and Claire bought was on a half-acre of land. They had to cross a neighbor's property to get to their place. The day they moved in, the neighbor woman said, "I just hope that house isn't cursed. The last two couples lived in it two years and then—fini. Good luck."

It turns out that Claire has *tried to be with women before.* That's the way she talks about it. All of that happened in her younger days, when she was a student. In Madison she had eaten magic mushrooms and found herself in bed with a woman named Leigh who wore rose-colored glasses. She told these stories self-mockingly, as if to reassure Ellen. That was then, this is now. She said that later she figured out that there was no chemistry with Leigh—being in the same bed in the wee hours of the morning was just an idea one of them had. Then there was a teacher she felt a keen attraction to; this story had a bit more edge to it. When Claire spoke of the teacher—Diana—her voice thickened with the memory of lust.

Would Ellen someday be reduced to a self-deprecating story?

People—older people—often told these stories on themselves. She had never noticed it before. Her mother's stories had all been cautionary tales. But Claire and her professor friends, and Claire's older sister who sometimes drove up from Louisville, told stories that had no dire warnings attached to them. They were entertainment, confessions of youthful ineptitude. These stories were trotted out, often after the consumption of much alcohol. (Claire favored aquavit in a shot glass since she had learned from experience that its hangover was minimal.) The stories commanded rueful, ironic laughter. Ellen sensed that they looked askance at her, greenhorn in life.

Summers, Ellen's boss lets her take five weeks without pay to travel with Claire. With the students gone, there isn't much business. Some years they go to Greece or Italy. But for several summers Claire teaches in England. Ellen isn't sure why she loves it. It seems awfully much like home, with the dreary rain and the gray skies and the green pastoral byways.

This is eight years later. Claire is almost fifty. Ellen is thirty-one. The Internet has changed travel; you can't escape home. Someone is always emailing you with news. This very morning she has received a gossipy email from her mother: Tommy Mattingly's significant other (the animal companion professor) has been in a car accident. Their little girl was thrown from the car and miraculously bounced into some shrubs and emerged, as Ellen's mother said, without a scratch, although Ellen finds that hard to believe literally. Tommy's significant other is in the ICU at Methodist Hospital in Indy. They don't know if she will make it.

Ellen perches on a bleacher at an outdoor theater on the Thames in Oxford. It's muggy, the grand old trees seeming to hold in the fetid summer air. Claire is checking her email at a café near Odd Lots. Ellen wasn't able to snag the best seats and she can see a bit of rehearsal going on, a man on stilts practicing. It's *A Midsummer Night's Dream*. She remembers a gorgeous production of the play they saw at the Oregon Shakespeare Festival, which tends to have more spectacle than British Shakespeare. And Ellen, feeling childish, loves spectacle: elaborate sets and costumes. On stage in Oregon there had been a satiny swinging quarter moon, large enough to sit in. She wishes they had taken the coach into London to see a play indoors, to escape the summer weather. She fingers her ticket stub, takes it out of her jeans pocket. Along the bottom edge it reads: No Refunds in Case of Inclement Weather. How inclement would it have to be for someone to want a refund? Pouring, she decides. That will not happen tonight. It's merely sticky, hot. They are at a spot where the Thames is lazy, dark, laid over with a skin of insects. Directly in front of her, a hetero man attends to his date, squeezing her shoulder, grinning as if they share a secret. He is American; Ellen can tell from the way he spreads his legs wide, taking up more than his share of space in the tight quarters, as if his genitals need room to breath. His partner's hair is feathery, rust-colored, and Ellen thinks she'd like to reach out and fluff it. Their complicity makes her lonely; she hadn't known she was lonely until now.

Claire arrives. About the seats, she says, "Are these the best you could do?"

Tears seep into Ellen's eyes.

"Sorry, sorry," Claire says, "I don't mean to be cranky." She takes off her glasses and wipes them on her blouse hem. She's wearing a blouse with Asian details, cherry blossoms like you would see on Japanese paper, a sash under her breasts. Her slacks are red; her shoes are red.

There has been a shift in Claire's wardrobe in the last few months. They no longer look as if they go together, something Ellen always enjoyed: comfort clothes, Birkenstocks and jeans and hoodies. Claire has been shopping, trying on different styles, as if she thinks the clothes will make her new, make her someone else. She complains that—in the Midwest—clothes for women her age are dull. That phrase—a woman my age—crops up often.

The evening light fades to a dull purple, almost dark. Theater lights go up, pink and blue. "How *are* you?" Ellen says, hoping to find out what was so urgent at the cyber-café.

"It's Tommy's girlfriend," Claire says. "She's in the hospital."

She has not mentioned Tommy in a very long time, but she says his name now as if she thinks it every day or speaks it every day, as if Tommy is a constant in their lives.

"I know," Ellen says.

"How do you know?"

Ellen gives her look of disbelief: how else?

Claire says, "What'd she say?"

Ellen whispers what her mother has written, and Claire nods and sighs, as if to confirm it. She adds: "He's freaked out totally."

"Well, sure—" Ellen starts to say, but the play has begun. There is always that short period at the start of Shakespeare when she has to gear down and concentrate and get in the groove. She can't quite manage it this time. She fidgets, wondering about Claire and Tommy.

Claire's nieces from Louisville—little girls six and four—came to visit for a week in the spring. Several times, Claire took them out to the state park to play with Tommy's little girl, who is almost three. Ellen didn't think anything of it. Except later, after the nieces had been shuttled back to Louisville, Claire said, "I really miss those girls." And another time, "Let's talk about having kids again." But her voice sounded teasing, as if she did not quite trust herself to say it with a straight face. Ellen said, "Are you out of your mind? I'm used to things the way they are." She felt a pinch of panic at the thought of getting pregnant. Surely that part would fall to her. And she had learned that much about herself: she did not want her body taken over by it.

Still, Ellen has her own imagined detours like cartoon thought bubbles she tries to ignore, detours that might take her away from Claire and the life they have carefully created. She might meet someone from her past all grown up by now. Or move to New Mexico where she has been told the light is perfect for watercolor. The grown up person from her past is sometimes Gatling; she saw his band perform at the brewpub and he has filled out, a man now, and he still has that light in his eyes. What would it feel like to flirt with him? For flirting with Claire has fallen by the wayside; now she understands her mother better. Now she sees that committed relationships are the ultimate bait-and-switch. You flirt, you commit, and then the deliciousness becomes something else. She is only thirty-one and deliciousness has flown out the window.

At intermission, she says, "Do you want to call Tommy and see how she is?"

And Claire says, "I did."

A few days later, Tommy Mattingly's significant other dies. Everyone takes it hard. There are two memorial services and a permanent marker—a cross—is planted at the right angle in the gravel road where she rolled the car. Tommy and his daughter are seen around town, a truncated family configuration that startles people who have known him for a long time. He wipes her chin with a baby wipe outside the Ben & Jerry's. Everyone says how lucky it is that he is the caretaker at the state park and therefore he can care for his little girl at home, with only the occasional babysitter. Tommy Mattingly— who has been called a daredevil, a player, a rascal, a dangerous guy, a son of a bitch—now, in these new circumstances, garners sympathy from everyone. Even Ellen's mother, who emailed a full report.

Oxford of the tawny spires, the romantic Oxford, becomes just another dismal town. The gleam has gone off it. While Claire teaches at Oriel College, Ellen pretends to paint. She carries her kit to gardens and down the canal towpath where the backs of houses are frothy with plant life and practical with boats and equipment. She sets up and she sketches this and that, but her heart isn't in it. She misses Claire. The time they have left has the feel of something to get through. One night in bed, Claire says, "I'm not sure about anything."

Ellen says, "About what?"

"I'm going through a stage of some sort."

"A stage or a change?"

Claire reaches for the chain on the bedside lamp and turns off the light. Her moving even that far away elicits an urge to pull her back. Ellen rolls over and sniffs deeply of Claire's scent, which has always pleased her. Claire holds her. She says, "Not to worry, love. Not to worry." In spite of the intimacy of that *love,* Claire's tone is businesslike. It's the tone she might use in her office with a student who has overstayed his welcome.

At the end of summer when they return home from Oxford, Claire becomes Tommy's go-to person if he needs help with his daughter. Amy. Amy's needs are in ascendance. If Ellen and Claire have plans, and Claire happens to leave her cell phone lying around, Ellen surreptitiously turns down her ringer so that Tommy can't reach them and spoil their plans. What Ellen dreams is this: she and Claire are going to see a movie at the university, an outdoor movie, somehow reminiscent of that play on the Thames. Stickiness in the air. When they arrive, they have to search for seats. The seats are like lawn chairs. There is a flurry of excitement because the actor in the movie, an alumnus of the university, has promised to show up. There is a slight mix up about who wants to sit where. Claire ends up several rows away, and when Ellen tries to catch her eye, Claire does not respond. Ellen had wanted to see the movie *with* Claire, but they are separated. She wakes up from this dream and says, "We're separated."

At the window, in her chenille bathrobe, her back to Ellen, Claire says, "No, we're not."

But her shoulders tremble, the weeping rising from a core place. Ellen gets out of bed, the floor cool on her feet. She goes to the window and wraps her arms around Claire. Claire shrugs her away. "You can't help me," she says.

Outside, a tree looks blue in the light. It is a blue like smoke in the bar side of their favorite Japanese restaurant in the part of town across the river where you can still smoke. You have to get the angle right to see its blueness. The window screen is foggy with pollen. It's not the sort of tree they noticed when they first moved in. The coldest day that winter. In the deepest snow the movers could recall. Ellen misses the maple tree from her mother's house, the way it spread its leaves in fall like a glittery skirt, a last dance.

She misses that maple the way she misses her unspent youth. Why did she go to work with those women in Chicago when she could have done anything? She could have gotten a job in a sunny climate; she could have gone to that art workshop in France where the students swear they learn to truly see *what is*; she could have taken road trips; she could have fallen in love when boys wanted her to. Once she said this to Claire and Claire said, "Oh, me, too. I miss that wildness I can't pull off anymore. You get used to that. The Dalai Lama would probably say that's all in the void. Like last year's Super Bowl. I'll take his word for it."

And Ellen had cheerfully said, "God bless the Dalai Lama."

For they had been mysteriously close then. And now they aren't. Mysteriously.

The blue tree's limbs had been amputated after the tornado that hit the house the spring before they bought it. Yet it lumbers on, not a tree you'd put the word *sylvan* to, but still, she thinks it's growing. She reaches for Claire's hand and Claire lets her take it.

She wants to run to her mother and ask her to throw the I-Ching, or do a Tarot reading, but all that feels scary. Bad news waiting at the door. She wants to say, "Are you still thinking about kids?" Or: "Let's plan a trip for winter break." Or: "Do you want to throw a party?" Or: "Let's buy new skis." In her mind, they have equal weight: attempts to dispel Claire's unhappiness.

Finally, there is a night when Claire doesn't come home.

The next afternoon Ellen visits her mother and then she drives out to the state park, but not the old way, the way she used to go, before the park was built. She takes Swisher Road, by the gravel pit, and pays her fee at the brown booth. She parks near the replica of a 1920's farmhouse where a gaggle of school kids in the lee of a barn watch a park employee milk a cow. It's colder now, definitely not fall, but not quite winter. November. Not a time to be out after dark. The swath through the prairie garden is damp, squishy underfoot, and the wet seeps over the back of her clogs and the wetness wicks up her socks. The tansy is brown, soggy. All the maples have lost their leaves. But the sycamore leaves still cling like fat hands. She trudges, nearer and nearer Tommy Mattingly's house.

Vivian had laid out the Tarot cards on the government-issue desk at the PO, amid the gray mail bins, after she took down the flag. This card represents Amy, she said. And this card represents your paintings. Vivian didn't take pleasure in Ellen's heartache: that was a relief. She was clinical almost, like a surgeon. For several months Ellen had imagined her saying "I told you so." The reading felt interminable: this card, that card. The only card that stood out for Ellen was the one that represented Amy, what she was still denying. Ellen thinks *Amy* and the name is in a box in her imagination, not attached to an image of the girl. Not wanting to see the girl almost makes her turn back.

She keeps going until she spots them, tiny stick people, at the swing set. Tommy Mattingly pushes Amy in her swing. It's one of those baby swings, a plastic tub that the girl won't fall out of. Claire is settled on the bench of a picnic table, with both hands holding shut her quilted jacket. Wood smoke rises from the chimney of the caretaker's house. Ellen can smell it. A smell that under other circumstances might have been as comforting as newly baked bread. Still she draws nearer. Flapjack senses her and races out past the shed, tail wagging. Tommy Mattingly leans, ever so tentatively, toward Claire. She hugs him to her, presses her face into his belly. They look up at Ellen but they do not pull away from each other guiltily. Later Ellen will think: What they have is so pure that they didn't even feel guilty when I walked up. She is determined to think the best of other people. A fault, according to her mother. Years later, after she has betrayed someone, she'll know better. She'll know that love is stronger than guilt. Not that it's pure, only stronger. Flapjack is at her feet, sniffing, shivering, smiling the way dogs do. She walks on. The little girl shouts, "Fappy, Fappy," what she calls the blind dog. Her pink angora cap has slipped off and lies in the mulch. She pumps her legs and beats the side of the swing with her fist. "Go, go." The air has weight that's different from early fall: wet, sad. Ellen is crying. Claire rises to embrace her, to set her free.

KAPUT

THIS HAPPENED RIGHT AT THE START of what people call the downturn. They make it sound like a temporary condition, like a particularly harsh winter, but I am not so sure.

I thought I'd woken up in California. It was 1957. I was older than I would have been then. Stan Kenton was on the radio. The louvered windows were cranked open. It was before plastic bags were used in grocery stores. All food was whole food. I was un-schooled, but I had an intellectual life. That is to say, I used the public library. Every day until noon I wore a slinky robe. Then I went to work at a bookstore or a record store. Selling something—that was the feeling. I liked men. It did not matter that I had small breasts. They said, "Anything more than a mouthful is wasted." Later I would stop believing that they were sincere. I was not a vir-gin, but I could remember what it felt like to be a virgin. There was a pan-asian-y feel to everything, very Pacific Rim, with the ceiling fan blades a smoky red lacquer.

That lasted about six seconds. Then I was back in Ohio, on the edge of a defunct liberal arts college. Waking up in my van. Without my job. The number-crunching job I had loved, in the financial aid office at the selfsame liberal arts college. Thinking, "Frank Zappa said that, so it can't be 1957." The redbud trees had begun to bloom, but it was near freezing when I unfolded my ach-ing fifty-eight-year-old bones and got out of the van to the March daybreak. Frost skinned over the down parka I'd forgotten to bring in. It lay on a picnic table, a creamy white, flattened cadaver. They had stopped cutting the grass the summer before. That's how all the worker bees had known the college was about to shut down. I had to choose a place to pee, always the first order of business

when you live in your van. Alex, my ex, lives in California. A fore-
man at a wind farm. Was that where such a full-blown, unbidden,
California half-dream had come from? Was it about Alex?

So far as I knew, no one had put together an intervention. No
one had slyly asked me to save a date, the way they would for a
surprise birthday party. No one had yet come right out and said:
What the hell are you going to do? You're almost sixty years old.
(I'm not! I wanted to say. Fifty-eight is fifty-eight!) And you have
already spent your paltry retirement savings on five months in Europe. Under every encounter lay this worry: Will I have to rescue
you? My daughter Willow would leave the room exasperated, spitting out "Boomers—." I wasn't simply her mother who had lost her
job. I represented a generation of people about to enter their golden
years unprepared. Willow, Alex, and my friend Kim all thought that
I had swerved over the line and hit those hard dots on the highway
that remind you: hey, get with it, you're asleep at the wheel.

Kim had sent me a ticket to Mexico. Free! For points! Willow
disapproved. She had said, reasonably, "Mom. You've *got* to stop
traveling. You're on unemployment. Jesus, Mary, and Joseph, as
Aunt Mina would say."

Amid overgrown ornamental grasses, behind the library, I
squatted and remembered all this, and the day seemed brighter.
I would fly from Columbus to Cancun. Kim would meet me and
take me to her home in Puerto Morelos. To get my head together.
Kim still talked like that. With Kim you got your head together,
things were trippy or a bummer, you got a wee bit wasted.

We hadn't seen each other in over thirty years, and we were riding around in her champagne-colored hybrid SUV that had her
trademark—youblossom.com—stencilled on both front doors. All
those years, the phone and then email had been equalizers. As if
we hadn't been through ugly times, power plays. On the phone we
were all "hello, sweetie," and "take care."

After we stopped at the Cancun Costco and were out on the
highway, she said, "Is everything all right?"

"Why wouldn't it be?" I said.

She popped in a Jimmy Buffett CD. One time long after the divorce, Alex and I had taken Willow to a Jimmy Buffett concert in Angels Camp. We drank syrupy margaritas someone handed us in plastic cups. Willow was only five and happy that Mom and Dad were having fun with her. She knew the words to most of the songs. Alex was still with Kim—the outing was covert.

She said, "You just seem…"

The highway out of Cancun was like a kids' board game, with signage every few yards. Beaches, beaches—this way pleasure lies.

Meekly, I said, "We've been building a bridge, right?" We had talked every three months for the last fifteen years.

"Sure."

"I thought—when I saw you—that the last little bit of the bridge would click into place." I had to catch my breath, as if I'd said too much. "But there's still a gap."

"Don't look down," she said. Her tone all-wrong. Bitchy? Playful? That is, I felt serious. My life somehow depended on what would happen in the next week.

By early evening we were strolling on the beach, navigating the blue-and-white striped beach umbrellas under which die-hards sipped their evening cocktails. In the shallow sea, French Canadian toddlers squealed, "Ma*ma*." And on the far horizon, the pearly gray of cruise ship exhaust. I wore a swirly skirt and a top that provided plenty of infrastructure. I had forgotten how much we looked alike. I remembered Kim as plump in a sexually ripe sort of way, with hair the color of cow's cream down to her waist. Now we matched: short, tightly-exercised, with good biceps and silvery hair, our faces sun-mottled and blurry with fine lines, flaunting post-tennis swaggers, even though we didn't play tennis. We were perky, as if to prove something to the world. We're not old. Basically that was the message. Now, could Alex have told us apart from a distance?

*　　　*　　　*

It was awkward to say, but I always describe Kim as "the woman Alex was with after me." Alex and Kim had lasted long enough to have two boys. They work in the solar panel industry. I relayed Willow's latest scheme—she and her partner were starting up a franchise of garages that would convert gas hogs to electric. It must be genetic, this obsession with energy issues. The soft, gray beach sand grew clammy beneath our bare feet. We talked about the kids in shorthand. We knew all about the school problems, the boy-girl problems, the trophies won, the AP courses, the applications for college, the best and worst significant others, the moves, the resume-building and the jobs. Kim and I liked to say that we were almost blood relatives, but the final word on the kids was this: They have their own lives.

Then we touched on the parents, what we already knew. At that time, hers were in assisted living near Emory, where her father had worked for over forty years. "They still play bridge," she said. Was that a speck of one-upmanship? Mine had passed away within months of each other while Reagan was still president. To remember their faces I have to dig up curling Kodak photos from a shoebox in Willow's attic. The scent of Shalimar or something in the grocery—Underworld Deviled Ham—might remind me. A twinge of loss.

"Let's stop here for dinner," Kim said. We stood before an impromptu fish house, plastic tables and chairs set amid the sand slaloms. Solar torches lit the way. The food came forth from a concrete block building with a corrugated metal roof. Wind blew off the Caribbean. My skirt flipped over my face, my white, northern legs exposed. An empty table tumbled away; the wind was that strong. The sky was the color of lilacs.

I hesitated.

"It doesn't look like much," Kim said, "but they have a chef from New Orleans." Then, "My treat."

"I'll get it next time," I said. My debit card still worked. Which is to say, I had some money in the college credit union. At home, I kept a close eye on the balance. In a notebook, I wrote down every single dollar I spent or withdrew. I'd had an overdraft incident the month before and Willow had grudgingly sat down at a computer and helped me sort it out. As if I'd lost my number-crunching gift.

"Whatever, honey," Kim said. "Not to worry." She had taken up the habit of calling everyone *honey* or *sweetie.* I thought it was from living in Atlanta before she moved to Mexico.

That was the last time Kim had to say, "My treat." After that, it was understood that almost everything we did was her treat. I held up my end feebly by purchasing fruit at the market, washing it, and stacking it artfully in a ceramic bowl on the kitchen counter.

That evening, before the walk on the beach, people had come to the door to be paid. At first I couldn't make out who they were. But Kim's voice altered when she talked with them. She was managerial, but kind.

Kim did not have to worry about being unemployed. She employed other people. A housekeeper, a gardener, a Mayan errand boy with industrial-looking metal braces on his teeth that Kim had paid for. He was a senior. Eventually he would go forth with a blazing smile and a high school diploma, the first person in his family to finish. And why didn't I know about these people? How would she have told me? Oh, by the way, I have *servants.* People who do my bidding. Minions.

I pictured myself working for her. At a computer. Helping people make their dreams come true. Helping people *blossom.* All that crap. Wearing a nice outfit every day, even though Kim worked in yoga pants or pajamas. Her house was whitewashed, blocky, two stories, with five bedrooms. A view of the sea. And a cheerful kitchen paved in blue-and-yellow tiles. The garden ran amok with birds-of-paradise and hibiscus and palm trees. Kim had made her most recent pile of money as a motivational speaker. Now she did not even have to show up. She maintained a website and her clients paid to chat and ask her questions. She offered a Kim-style brew of astrology, creative visualization, and financial planning.

In the middle of the night, I'd pad barefooted across the clean tile floor to my own clean bathroom to pee. Because I could. Because I didn't have to lie awake in my van, my bladder full as a water balloon, forcing myself to get up, get out. New-age music, lobotomy music, fluttered faintly twenty-four/seven. When I got back into the queen bed, I'd lie awake in the creature comfort of the bedding, the scents—clean cotton and curry or hot peppers from our evening meal. I'd think about what to keep on the downlow. The Jimmy Buffett concert. Sex with Alex two months before when I went to see him in California. I don't know why I did that. Or why I wouldn't want her to know. She had told me years ago that the thought of being physical with Alex gave her the heebie-jeebies. We did it on a vinyl couch in a maintenance building at the wind farm, with the turbine blades cutting through the batter of the wind. Our bodies did not work the way they once had. I just missed him. Missed having a man's broad back to encircle with my arm at night. Then, there was that crush I had on Henry Gravitt when Kim and Alex were getting together. At the time I had some virtuous-sounding reason for not telling Alex. Rock bottom, I wanted to play the aggrieved party. That had been my take-away from six years of therapy.

Halfway through my visit, we got tarted up for blues night at the Chinese restaurant. We set out on foot, into the dusk. I did not want to think about money or talk about money or make money plans. But Kim loved to talk about money. Money and people from our jolly, sordid past. I would ask, What about Jumper? What about Sugar? What about Georgette? What about Sequoia? Kim was the keeper of newsy bits. Why didn't I know what she knew? And worse, what did she tell them about me? At the plaza, girls in tight jeans rehearsed a dance routine for carnival. Music stirred the air: salsa and Mexican ballads. Tiny white lights hung in loops along the eaves of the Chinese restaurant. Right before we went inside, Kim leaned against me. In my ear she whispered a dig: "Lighten up." I had to blink back tears.

Faux-paper lanterns gave off a copper glow on the back patio. It was packed. Vast steaming quantities of shrimp and noodles and broccoli lay before the diners. We settled at a round table, already sticky. You had to shout to talk. The amps outsized the space. *She my sweet little thang.* What would I do to lighten up by Kim's standards? Dance by myself? Order two martinis? Get on my goo-goo eyes?

Kim invited a man in aviator glasses to join us. Right away she moved up front with a video camera to record the band for

YouTube, leaving me with the man—Russell. The music was so loud—at first I had to read his lips. He scooched closer. I could smell his aftershave. He had a sun-scarred face, a long white pony-tail, and a slightly southern accent. His voice sort of reached into me. I felt a lick of attraction. Just go with it, I thought. Russell held court, giving me a crash course on himself. Five years in the Air Force. Later, he had a high-tech job at a regional airport. Worked his way up through the union. Believed in unions, the people who brought you the weekend. He had returned from Cuba only the day before. In Cuba, men and women alike propositioned him every day. He said, "It's the one thing Fidel cannot control." I said, "And so?" He shook his head distastefully, but bragged about the salsa moves he had perfected. He seemed like a man for whom little had gone wrong. He was a talker and that was a relief. I did not have to tell him that the plates on my van would expire in three weeks and that I could not afford to renew them. No need to reveal the ins and outs of all that. No. To him, I was a fresh slate.

Kim darted back to the table. She pointed a finger at him like a pistol and said, "The last time I saw you was carnival—Merida." So she knew him. I was the outlier, the *extrana*. For a while we volleyed, vied for his attention. In the caterwaul we told stories on ourselves. Tidy stories, familiar.

Russell went off to the men's room. Kim was a wiggler in her seat when there was live music. Out of the blue she shouted, "You heard about Lindsay, of course."

"Lindsay?" I shouted back. And that is when she told me Lindsay Gravitt had committed suicide at the farm by slitting her own throat.

Alex and I hadn't been hippies or hedonists. We had regular jobs before we moved to the anarchist farm. I worked in my father's drugstore. Alex worked at a water pump station. He understood watersheds and global warming and biologically active mud. He always knew what phase the moon was in. All of that was new to me and perplexing. Which is to say, I admired him for it, but I chafed under his constant instruction. Seasonally, he worked in an orchard that belonged to his Aunt Mina. This was in the hillocky southeast corner of Ohio, a few miles from a small town with one stoplight. Our rental house had architectural flourishes. There was a carport with white wrought iron supports that I thought were tacky until I lived at the farm with no shelter for my car.

My crush on Alex started when my mother thought I was too young to have a crush. Pre-puberty, at a time when I still played with dolls. We lived up the lane from Aunt Mina and I noticed him chugging by on the rusted-out tractor. I noticed his tanned arms, the rakish tilt of his baseball cap. Now I think about how inexplicable lust is. Alex has a short forehead with a little dent in the middle. He was going bald, even then.

Once they turned fourteen, girls worked in the orchard after school and on the weekend—picking ginger golds and winesaps. Alex advised his aunt to hire girls. They didn't goof off the way boys did. At lunch he'd sit amid them, under an apple tree, passing around ice water and homemade brownies and whatever else the girls had baked the night before. He would sprawl there, legs wide, grinning.

I pined after him. When my time came, I worked my tail off. We flirted. We made out in the barn. When I graduated from high school, we were married at the Catholic Church in town. I had to promise I would raise our children Catholic. That was fine. After the wedding, nothing mattered but getting Alex into that hotel room in downtown Cincy and finally going all the way. We had done everything but. It did not disappoint me. I fantasized the other girls hovering on the periphery, their envy. I was that young.

Being married felt sweet, ordinary. We established that ordinariness. But it turned out Alex had dreams he hadn't told anyone. It was as if being married gave him access to them. He wanted to change the way things were headed. He fretted about energy and overpopulation. "Bonnie, Bonnie, Bonnie," he'd say, "the world's a mess." Whenever Alex hunched at the supper table, telling me his worries, I had to concentrate hard to understand it all. He was educating me, but it wasn't an education I'd chosen. Now that I've sampled college courses like a smorgasbord for years, I'm wise to that.

On Saturdays when Alex worked the orchard, I would keep Aunt Mina company, shelling peas or cutting quilt pieces. Alex said he didn't want me to have to work in the orchard. I would drift to the window, tuck back the curtain, and watch the girls arriving on their bicycles. I wished I were among them. Barely eighteen, I had crossed over to another realm. I noted their short-shorts, which ones had dimpled thighs already, which ones were busty.

Aunt Mina and my mother were different. Visiting Aunt Mina you took a few steps back in time. She wears a *sun*bonnet, for crissakes, Alex would say. Like a frontier gal. She dated—men in town liked her. There was a fireman, a mortician. After I had begun junior high, my mother had gone for her real estate license and her first plastic surgery. A bitter, angular woman, every day she wore high heeled shoes that tortured her feet.

Now when I have reason to talk about those years at the anarchist peace farm, I say, "We moved out to the country. I wanted to be like Aunt Mina. Generous. Earthy. Not like my mother." I keep it vague. The details get plowed under—sending away for the magazine about intentional communities, composing the hand-written letters to apply, receiving enticing letters and photographs back, all of it taking months, and then the big yard sale at which we divested ourselves of electric appliances and frivolous items we'd been given as wedding presents, the trek across the country in a VW bus when gas was only fifty cents a gallon, the shock of driving down into the canyon, the mind-altering substances (marijuana, home-brew, LSD, magic mushrooms, you name it), the drama of living with thirty-seven other people.

Aunt Mina would never have done the things I did at the farm.

Aunt Mina would never in a million years have stood naked under an outdoor shower while a friendly neighbor man called out, "Must be jelly 'cause jam don't shake like that."

Alex and I had been married almost five years. It was a different time. People didn't move around like crazy. At first my mother was put-out. Then grief set in. Her only daughter was moving to the western edge of the continent. We were not caught up in the romance of a back-to-the-land life: growing organic food and making do. The big thing, the really big thing, I told my mother as she dabbed tears away with a handful of tissues, was that Alex had all these ideas about inventions that would save the world. His A.A. degree was in wastewater treatment. He had a shed full of pipes and wrenches and diagrams. He wanted to build a methane generator so that when you shit—went to the bathroom, I said to my mother—the gasses would in a twinkling make electricity to run your small appliances. The very appliances we had sold at the yard sale. This was in 1973.

Our cabin—built of scavenged lumber and bricks—was a $500 bargain. The boy who built it used the money to finance a trip to the Andes to apprentice himself to a sorcerer. There was a rule at the farm that you could not sell your home for any more than the cost of the materials. I decided I was a quilter, even though I'd never done more than cut neat stacks of diamonds and rectangles for Aunt Mina. I ground organic wheat and baked bread. I bartered this and that. I got a part-time job at a drugstore. All for Alex and his methane generator dreams.

I had a secret.

Alex was a natural-born flirt and I was sick with jealousy nearly every day we were together. I grew accustomed to it, like a sore that won't heal. The new normal, someone on TV might say today. After I married Alex, jealousy was the new normal.

What we never discussed before the move to the farm was the lure of free love. We knew about it, but I couldn't think the phrase without what my therapist called protective irony. After five years, my fantasies of my high school friends watching me have sex with Alex had faded. I was only twenty-three. Sometimes at night, the fire banked, the kerosene lamp a sheen by which to read or sew, satisfaction was unavoidable. Then lickety-split I'd wonder, "Is this all there is?" If Alex were in the shop working, I might put on several layers of winter clothing and trudge through the squeaky snow to a neighbor's house. We would stay up half the night talking. It might seem unnecessary to reverse the process and walk home. I might sleep on that neighbor's sofa. Sleeping over made me feel like a girl again. I wanted something: I wanted to crave something.

*   *   *

Henry Gravitt and his sister Lindsay drove down into the canyon in a truck from the fifties painted the color of limes. A home paint-job. It was summer when they arrived, full of plans and enthusiasm. They had cash from Lindsay's divorce. Henry had been in school, a poet. He wore a suit—linen pants and a double-breasted jacket he said he had paid a Thai tailor to make custom. It was ratty from traveling, but elegant. His hair was blond. It fell fetchingly across his forehead. He had that gene—now I know there is a gene for it—that enabled him to pick up on the needs of others. A communicator. He might have made a good politician, but he was an anarchist-poet. Lindsay did not seem right, even then. They moved into a hogan not far from our cabin.

I did not believe in love at first sight until Henry. My crush on Alex had developed over time, like a sickness that can't be diagnosed right away. When Henry got out of the lime-green truck, near the mailbox on the main road, I clutched a handful of mail and was about to head back to my cabin. I had an outdoor fire going. I was canning cherries in the front yard. My clothes and hands and face were sticky with cherry juice, my hair matted with it. My baggy shorts and T-shirt stained like pale rosy continents on a map. I longed for a shower or a dip in the creek.

Tickled, self-congratulatory, Henry said, "We have arrived."

When I heard his voice, I felt as if I'd had a brain transplant. Calmly, I said, "Welcome." But I wanted to reach out and touch him. Jump his bones, as we used to say.

Then Lindsay got out of the truck. Amazonian, in a sundress and delicate sandals. Her face and arms slightly sunburned, her nose peeling. The sundress was printed with tiny sprigs of mint. Lindsay laughed. She threw her arms up toward the canyon walls. Her armpits had been recently shaved. Ditto, her legs. She said, "So this is it. End of the road." That was probably the last time I heard Lindsay laugh. That very day her mood turned upside down. They did not have running water. She would be hauling water in two-gallon white buckets until an overland gravity-fed system of PVC pipes might be installed.

The sun beat down malevolently—it was in the nineties, July. But we stood there. I fanned myself with a seed catalog. Flies zeroed in on me, keen on the cherry juice. Henry and Lindsay had, through the mail, purchased the hogan, within a creaking windbreak of Doug firs, up a ravine. They had driven from a suburb of Chicago in three days. A veneer of suburbia was evident on Lindsay—clean, neat, shaven. Henry, too, had shaved. Lindsay's toenails were polished pink.

I craved Henry. I wept at night for want of him.

It seemed as if Alex did not notice. I taught Henry and Lindsay what they needed to know to survive. How to start a fire in their wood cookstove. How to brew and bottle beer. How to dry fruit on screen doors laid flat over sawhorses. Whenever I came within a few feet of Henry, my body buzzed. He educated me, as well. He sometimes carried a sweat-stained book of poems in the back pocket of his work pants. I asked to borrow the books and Henry took to reciting poems whenever we worked together. For a long time after, at the library I would cruise the 811s.

There was a cow co-op, six families with one cow—Bessie. I urged Henry to join. I volunteered to work side by side with him in the barn. How I trembled as I went out into the still-dark summer morning to join Henry down the lane for dairy duty. He would recite "Fern Hill" as we worked. At Bessie's teats, my fingers brushed his.

Lindsay Gravitt was troubled. She loved more than anything a trip to the dump. There, wearing high rubber boots to protect herself from rats, she would forage for discarded makeup and skin products—nail polish, powder, lotions, and mascara. These she organized on shelves in her kitchen. You had to be careful—she might insist on giving you a makeover. Nudity we were used to. There were nude volleyball games and sauna parties. But Lindsay might be discovered wandering the main road at night, dressed only in combat boots. If she found a dead animal—a blue jay or a snake—she'd bring it home and let it dry in the crook of a cottonwood tree. In her garden she grew an overabundance of herbs but few root veggies, what you really needed to get through the winter. She had a pet rooster named Kerouac who terrorized anyone who ventured past a certain point on the path to the hogan. Still, she was charming. She always came bearing muffins she'd baked or a bundle of fresh lemongrass. In the wan oily light of a kerosene lamp, she would unfold a paisley scarf and read your Tarot cards, her voice husky and patient.

While I nursed my crush on Henry, Alex and Kim were hell bent on what they called *ending the tyranny of marriage* and *inclusiveness* and *openness.* That is, they wanted to have sex in the parsnip patch. They wanted to have sex in our bed. And why didn't I go for Henry, I wonder even now? Tit for tat? Or, as some people might have thought, Why not give Alex a dose of his own medicine?

One day Lindsay found an airtight blue plastic drum at the dump. She donated it to Alex's project. I saw her going into the shop and I saw her coming out, shielding her eyes from the sun with one hand. She looked like a woman who had gone to a movie in the middle of the day and emerged from the theatre having forgotten that it was daytime. As if she'd been somewhere. She wore only a cotton petticoat, one strap falling off her shoulder. She picked her way down the path to my front porch. I went out to the porch, drying my hands on a dishtowel. I was pregnant with Willow by then, my belly big under Alex's bowling shirt left over from Ohio. Up close there was something pathetic about Lindsay. She did not bathe well. One side of her neck was gray, like a paw print. She had stopped polishing her toenails. Still, she was undeniably beautiful.

She stood her ground in front of my porch, in the pine duff.

"How's every little thing?" I said.

"He's attracted to me," she said.

A crackle of irritation and jealousy lit me up. "Get out of here, Lindsay," I said. "Just go."

And she did. She turned tail and went. Shooed away like a stray dog.

At the end of blues night, after too much Argentine wine, Russell put a hand possessively on the back of Kim's neck. She tilted her head toward him. Wattle, wattle, I thought, noticing hers for the first time. The sound of the word in my mind almost made me laugh. I had a key to the house. I said, "Bon voyage. I'll catch a taxi." Kim made a fuss over me and Russell stood by, waiting.

At the house, I attempted to sober up with two aspirin and a glass of orange juice. I checked my email. I went to the farm's website and tried to recognize the faces of the picnickers gathered under a maple tree. I remembered that tree. The sofa seemed like a good place to wait for Kim, a cushiony nap-friendly sofa. The sea swish-swished, but remorse about Lindsay would not let me fall asleep.

Hours later, Kim tiptoed in. I sat up alert, with a killer head-ache and questions. She put a kettle on to make tea. I knew that moment from the farm, that turn in the road where you decide to stay up all night or as long as it takes.

Jumper, a longtime farm resident, had emailed the news to Kim. Jumper had said that the blood—pints and pints of it—seeped into the mattress, a darkening stain by the time they found her. It was all over the place, on the wall, the floor. He did not know why she chose that house, that bed. The man whose goats she was supposed to tend was a quiet, asexual guy who grew fields of garlic and built birdhouses to sell in the city. The goats bleated from the pain of not being milked. That's why she was found when she was. There was an open book facedown on the bed, a Norwegian novel titled *Kristin Lavransdatter*. The sheriff had to come, and that had happened very seldom. They avoided turning to the authorities when things went wrong.

And things had gone wrong. There had been truck accidents, houses burned down. There had been thievery. And domestic vio-lence. Once a baby had died. But this took the cake, Kim said. Why would she? In her fifties, when life tends to get better. Speak for yourself, I said, and she laughed.

I said, "What did I care if she'd slept with Alex? It might have made a difference to her."

"What're you talking about?"

"Sexual healing. All that jazz."

Kim leaned closer, her voice an incredulous warble. "Lindsay wanted to sleep with Alex?"

I had a little bauble she coveted, a story impinging on her story. "I told her to get lost," I said.

"Don't be too hard on yourself," she said. Her stock advice.

I had not thought about Lindsay Gravitt in years.

Later that night I asked Kim if she had a job for me. She said she'd been thinking about it.

It was nearly daybreak. She went first, up the outdoor stairway at the abandoned house, reaching back for my hand. *Will you still need me, will you still feed me,* I sang to myself. Her hand was soft, lotioned. Wind knocked a lawn chair over on the patio down below. Weeds grew a foot tall out of the cracks in the cement. She let go of my hand and struggled with the key. When she opened the door it smelled bad inside. A dead animal and maybe mildew. We went in. She switched on the overhead light. The mattress was stained. I didn't want to think with what. A cracked sliding glass door led to a smidge of balcony. One blade of the ceiling fan had snapped off. CDs without cases lay strewn around the room. I wanted to check out the CDs but stooping to pick them up would have looked too much like trash picking. "You can see the water from here," she said. Another saving grace was the bathroom, with a walk-in shower and a ceramic sink painted with birds. Out the side window, in shadow, a boy and girl lay half-dressed on the rooftop next door. They curled tenderly on a blanket beside a satellite dish. It made me melancholy, and then cross, to think of how far I was from passion. Cross because I didn't want to care about that.

"A fixer-upper," I said.

"Can't you see it?" she said. "A boutique hotel. Only eight rooms."

"I can see it."

All business, Kim went around the room straightening the fake art, pictures of Mayan ruins and seashells. Later, she would toss them out in the rubbish. Her back to me, she said, "I want to get it renovated—off the runway—by the end of hurricane season."

Palm trees whipped against the balcony railing. I went into the bathroom, on the pretense of examining its features. A frisky lizard the size of my thumb dashed into the shower.

"You can live here," she said. "I need someone to supervise the job—start to finish."

"What about your place?"

"Oh, Bonnie, honey, my astrologer tells me I'm meant to live alone."

Her astrologer told her that her mother was a porcupine in another life. Her astrologer told her to move to Mexico. Her astrologer told her to offer me a job.

A front was called for. What was one more front? I missed my van, my autonomy, such as it was. The empty, dilapidated campus I thought of as my own estate. I missed the lonely security cop who would tell me to keep an eye on things while he scurried on foot across the state highway to Mary Lou's Doughnuts. He'd bring us back warm apple fritters and coffee as thin as green bean juice.

I said, "First things first—I'll need a curtain."

"We can go to Costco and get whatever you need."

I said, "What a generous offer." For now, it'll do for now. Who knew where it would lead? Out on the balcony, a skinny white cat stretched, arching her back, just waking up. "I need a cat," I said.

"And a cat you shall have," Kim said, as if she had produced the cat from up her sleeve.

She smiled, a crafty, self-satisfied grin. I recognized it. Once I'd come upon her and Alex tucked into the outdoor bathtub, soaking in hot water. Their bodies striped with moonlight. He did not see me, but she did. She closed her eyes and pretended otherwise. She straddled Alex, giggling, as he held her hips and entered her. It was the same grin. The better-than-you-grin.

SICILIAN KISSES

BARBARA AND COLIN TIDD met at the green show for *Macbeth*. Ashland, Oregon, 1977. They spent three years toing-and-froing undecidedly about marriage, tramping the Cascade Range, rain or shine. She worked in her parents' storefront gallery—Crossed Destinies. He drove over the mountains to a technical school to become a diesel mechanic. He had grown up in Whitehorse and, in bedtime whispers, he told Barbara that he wanted to move back to Canada. At last they married, in a rose garden. She changed her name to his and they moved to Echo, British Columbia, where the sex, which had been lively, did not—ka-boom—come to an abrupt end, but tapered off. Don't be surprised this time, her mother had warned, but she was.

Colin took a job at a garage that made emergency trips within a 500-kilometer range to rescue truckers and big rigs. Barbara had an irrational, hormonal response to men in blue-collar work garb. They seemed competent in the extreme, as if they could right any wrong, fix any household failure, or save you from sure death in the wilderness. Colin was stubby, but muscular. He shaved every day and scrubbed the oil and grit from his fingernails with a bar of Lava. If they were headed out to a trail, a river, or a reenactment, he was inordinately cheerful and eager. Reenactments were his true love; black powder buffs gathered in parks every few months to reenact history, particularly the killing. The men would reenact killing wild game, and—wearing layers of handsewn muslin and canvas and leather clothes, abundantly fringed and sometimes beaded, depending on whether you saw yourself as Indian or white—the women would reenact tomahawk throws and cooking venison and elk meat in big black kettles over open fires.

Barbara, years later, is an aspiring vegan, with honey and eggs all that she consumes from animals, but when she lived in Canada, meat was a staple, a symbol. She and Colin had a freezer full of elk, venison, bear, goat, salmon. The goat stank to high heaven, a smell like you might find outside a men's room in a bus station, as if his testosterone-laden spirit inhabited the cabin every time she cooked him. Even then she was mulling over: Why do we eat the flesh of other beings?

Colin's boss owned the cabin she and Colin lived in. That was considered temporary, until they got on their feet. They had moved to Echo—gone through the wedding and her tedious immigration paperwork—because they wanted to live on the edge of the wilderness. They reenacted timeworn notions about marriage, what she thinks of now as nostalgia. She would follow him; he would shoot or catch what they needed to eat. 1980 this was, she always says, not 1880. She'd traded her wedding gown for a Nikon F3 and that was to spare her from total invisibility, from evaporating, from being subsumed by her role in the reenactment.

It was Barbara's second marriage. She had not been subsumed by her first husband, a sociology professor; only twenty when they married impulsively at the courthouse, she'd been a scrapper and, according to him, deviant, with little urge to protect hearth and home. She would stay out all night with friends, perennial boys and girls, eating magic mushrooms. She painted peace signs on her forehead for rock concerts.

All of that seems almost quaint by today's standards of deviance. Look at the CAKE website. All-night events in New York. Girls on girls, half-naked, in a dance club. Porn marathons. Or even the dances the high school kids do—her friends have told her about it, her friends with children. She sometimes rationalizes what she did—she was young, that era was a foolish free-for-all—but then she remembers the grand, brutal fights she and the professor had before it ended. She took Halcyon for two months to keep from crying herself to sleep. There had been no divorce in her family. Her parents never got over it.

That second time, in Canada, she wanted to do right. She

churned her own butter and considered buying baby chicks. Labor-intensive effort was the norm in Echo. They were stouthearted people, the men like moose, the women tough but sexy. Country music twanged from pickup radios. Black bears came down into the village and ate the apples from the trees.

Mavis Ryan was the boss's wife. Surrounded by curls that seemed false as a doll's hair, her face was pink, moist, and Colin said her lips had a touch of the obscene about them, like a monkey's privates distended and presented for monkey business. Barbara could not speak to her ever again without remembering that and she disliked him for it, a feeling she hadn't noticed often in the three years they'd been together. She wondered if moving was bringing out the worst in him somehow.

Amid the moving rubble, Mavis came to visit several times the first week, with a local telephone book thin as a steno pad, gossip meant to feel her out, news of herself—she was from Victoria, too good for Echo—and blunt questions.

"So how old're you and Colin, ey?"

"I'm twenty-eight," Barbara readily told her. "And Colin's twenty-four."

"I could never marry a younger man," Mavis said sternly.

Good you don't have to, Barbara thought, but she said nothing.

On Friday Mavis told her about the belly dancing. Every woman within a twenty-kilometer radius of Echo belonged to a belly dancing class. She made it sound part therapy, part fitness routine, part coven.

Barbara said, "I like to swim. Is there a public pool?" She thought of the Y back home, the billowy turquoise chamber of the pool, how calm she was, how otter-like and svelte, when she did her morning laps to stay trim.

Until she met Colin, her swim had been the main event of the day after she moved back with her parents. Her girlhood room had been turned into storage for framed art. She had said it didn't matter; she went to sleep on her side with a lithograph of Aurora, Goddess of the Dawn, inches from her face. Her parents lived on the hill in Ashland with a sliver of mountains visible from the front porch. Even though Echo was embedded deep within mountains and she knew mountains were all around, you couldn't *see* them.

About the pool, Mavis laughed, almost cruelly. "You're out of luck," she said. "You're a country mouse now."

"They've invited me to belly dance," she said to Colin over supper that night. The boss had provided them with frozen cuts of last fall's venison and she had prepared a feast: little red garlicky potatoes and asparagus in butter and bread crumbs. A fruit pie for later. Colin loved a fruit pie. He would ask for pie instead of cake for his birthday.

"Belly dance?" He forked a slice of loin and held it aloft dramatically, a gesture that struck her as crude. They had lit a kerosene lamp, a burnished romantic light until he held the meat aloft. Too handsome for his own good, her mother had said early on, when she and Colin first dated; the phrase came back to Barbara.

"It's what they do. For fun. And exercise."

"Go ahead," Colin said, as if she needed his permission.

She shook her head. "I'm too clumsy." Two left feet, no rhythm, she thought, recalling the embarrassment—bordering on humiliation—of a modern dance class she'd taken a few years before: skipping erratically to Santana across a dimly lit gym in a leotard that didn't firm up a jiggle she'd been oblivious to before.

Furthermore, she didn't have the build for belly dancing. She was short, an "apple" her mother said, a shape that ran in their family. She had good legs and could wear short skirts well, so well that Colin, if he saw her in one, might corner her in the kitchen or a tavern parking lot and reach up her skirt. The full diaphanous skirts belly dancers wore would make her look like a spinster's bedroom lamp or a sea creature.

Still, friends might not come easily, if she didn't belly dance. People still deliberated whether to make a long-distance call, especially an international call, as if you might be a spendthrift for craving a voice from home. She received one bent-up postcard from a girlfriend who had gone on vacation to Catalina Island and a few letters from her mother—addressed to Mr. and Mrs. Colin

Tidd. Her subtext was clear. Don't forget you're married this time. After the cupboards had been scrubbed and everything put meticulously away, after she painted the bathroom spring green, she was hit with the thought, We *live* here. Her life in Echo would be a narrow constellation. Faded star to pale star she went, the cabin, the bank and grocery and library in town, a walk along the river with Colin on the weekend, the occasional reenactment. The idea that she might not make friends darted amidst her solitude, but then Lucy Givens appeared, bearing green tomatoes from her garden. "Please save these from the frost," she said.

Lucy mixed the Sicilian Kisses according to *The College Guide to Bartending*, a warped-from-rain hardcover book just the size to fit into the tight back pocket of some frat boy's jeans. One part Amaretto and one part Southern Comfort. On the rocks. Walking back to the cabin, Barbara would compose a list: what she liked about Lucy. The way she turned her face to the sun greedily. A slit-eyed sideways glance she bestowed, part seduction, part reprimand. Words she used: scrumptious, fiddledeedee, indecent, fetish, Pickwickian, darlin'. Her poppy red toenails. Her knees beneath snug jeans. Her kind, urgent nodding when Barbara had trouble spitting out what was on her mind. That she changed her earrings every day: studs, hoops, danglies. That she did not belly dance. The way, when they had gone to the lake, if the light were right, she would put on lipstick, just before going home. She'd fish an Avon sample from the coin pocket of her jeans, roll the lipstick on her lower lip and then smack her lips together. Then she'd take off her sunglasses and hold them up like a mirror to see if she'd gotten it on straight.

She—Lucy, of the Sicilian Kisses—had lived in Echo since junior high. She had four children, all in school but one, Isaac, the three-year-old. Her husband Matt was a skinny shitkicker (Lucy's words) who worked for the provincial road crew, laying blacktop and plowing snow. He would leave every morning around five-forty-five in a slurry of gravel, high-test coffee spraying out of his mug, his jeans so stiff with grime they might have stood up on their own. Barbara would watch him go. Conveniently, they lived across the road. By seven Lucy's children would be standing sleepy-eyed at the end of their driveway, waiting for the school bus.

By seven-thirty, Colin would be back from his jog in the woods, showered, and with a peck to her cheek, he'd leave for work. Barbara would skate on the silence for a bit, unglued by it. Right before leaving the States, they had lived near a bridge that buckled and banged day and night with the traffic's duress. She had gotten used to the noise, and she wondered now if the edge of the wilderness would ever feel secure.

Perhaps that was the point, Colin said—to always be on guard. When they met he had been astonished that Barbara, an Oregon girl, had never camped in the wilderness, never exposed herself to that risk. He initiated her; now she could build a dependable fire and put up a tent; she found uses for every tool on her Swiss Army knife. But in the silence she became convinced that bears lay in wait under the deadfall and in the woods surrounding the cabin. Or worse, maniacs gone mad from the silence.

To feel deserving of leaving the cabin, she would do the dishes, chop kindling, and carefully construct a crock pot dinner to brew during her absence—often a hunk of game fragrant with shallots and rosemary. Safety—emotional safety—was paramount, meaning she wanted no accusations. No name-calling. She had had enough of that to last a lifetime. Everywhere she went, she took her camera, for Colin approved of her goal and admired her work.

Isaac hated to see her coming. This should have been a clue of some kind, she tells her therapist. If animals and children are happy to see you coming, what you're about is probably charitable, good for everyone concerned. If not, you better wake up.

Isaac might've been eating Red River cereal at the kitchen table in his Superman pajamas, his copper hair bright as the bottom of a new saucepan, the rare picture of toddler quiescence, but when Barbara slipped in the back door—Lucy had told her early on not to knock—he'd frump and frown and throw his spoon at Gandolf, their nutmeg-colored mutt. When Lucy came into the room and said, "Thank God you're here," Isaac would whine, "You ruined it, Mommy." Meaning the morning. He'd say, scowling at Barbara, "I'm going to tee-tee on the floor."

Lucy would toss her the tin of Craven A tobacco and say, "Roll me one, would you?"

Brooding, Isaac would amuse himself with Matchbox cars and the two women would talk, talk, talk, while Lucy did her chores, indoors and out. She had chickens and goats; there were brown eggs to be gathered and a goat to be milked. There were leftover biscuits to be put away and counters wiped and floors swept. Her house was like a Carl Larsson watercolor, homey, cheerful, some earthy potpourri simmering atop the woodstove, the colors of her second-hand linens and furniture Swedish-pastel, chosen to ward off the chill of the long winters. She still used a wringer washer and did a couple of loads of laundry every day, shoving it over to the stainless steel kitchen sink, a cigarette dangling from her mouth. Her hands were raw from working and she disregarded them, although she put care into the rest of her looks. She hadn't given that up. Her hair was that same copper red, frolicking down her back with little effort. She wore her gloss of lipstick late in the day when Matt was due, but he didn't always come home when expected. He kept her keen like a falconer keeps his birds keen. Willowy, tall, Lucy hid behind baggy shirts Matt had discarded or a flannel-lined barn jacket she'd bought at a charity shop in Vancouver where her mother had taken her on a weekend holiday to celebrate her birthday. Freckles floated like a mask across her sharp face, vestige of her pregnancies. When she told you some truth she might not have spoken aloud before, her dark eyes narrowed and drilled home.

You might remember in *Drugstore Cowboy* when Dianne says to Bob, You never want to fuck me and you always make me drive. Lucy said that first, in 1980, about Matt. It must have been something going around in the Eighties, the reverse of silver lining. Her body wasn't the same, she said, after four babies. She'd been damaged in the place that matters most to men. Sex hurt. It's not what you hear from women, but it happens.

They spoke of the lofty and the profane, of books and movies and movie stars, the state of the world, the child-rearing practices of their parents, bands they wished they'd been groupies of, the sexual mores of cultures they would never know, the worst and best moments of their lives, how they'd like to change, how they'd like their husbands to change, who they'd fuck in the neighborhood, if there were no repercussions. Not a conversation Colin would approve of.

Two or three days a week, they would talk in Lucy's car, for privacy, once Isaac had been dropped off at her mother's for an afternoon of grandmotherly delights. She had mixed the Sicilian Kisses in a kids' school thermos with kelly-green kites all over it. Barbara drove, out of tenderness toward her. They would run a couple of errands so that they could claim to have been dutiful, if called to task, then they would drive out to the lake and burrow down a dirt lane through the red willows to a spot used by lovers on weekend nights. Lucy and Matt had probably used it themselves years before.

Barbara and Colin had camped at that same lake the night before they moved into the cabin. They had been eager to begin their new life, hopeful. The next morning, over a fire, he had heated water with which to shave. She had photographed him sitting on a canvas campstool, a mirror in one hand, a razor in the other, stripped to the waist, a towel across one knee. It had been a moment of pure love; if asked, she would not have been able to parse the moment into segments: her love of Colin, the mountain air, the loons calling. He had said, "I feel married now. We moved together. You being here makes my life better."

But, oh, the incandescent, unbearable things she and Lucy said—

The pines grew densely; the blackish-green shadows reflected in the deep water. Right before dark, which came precipitously—a rush of changing weather during early October, a warning—the light on the lake was violet. Time to go, time to go. "Such lucidity," Lucy would say, "cannot be borne for long." She would say that. She hadn't gone to college, but she'd read more than Barbara had. Her voice was gravelly, sugary.

When Colin first learned that she was spending entire days with Lucy, he said, "You've got too much time on your hands." "I'm shooting," she said. "That's all. She keeps me company." A lie that came so naturally, that burbled forth, balm on her anxiety. To keep the lie little and white, every so often she would take spontaneous shots of lichen or witch's butter, whatever grew randomly on logs and stones. Lifeless pictures that meant nothing to her.

Was it around this time that Barbara began to fear choking? She's not sure. It crept up on her. She denied it to herself. There were the half-eaten burgers shoved away, ice cream left melting in the bowl, beverages she would sip from and leave on the kitchen counter. Her throat would tighten; she would be excruciatingly aware of her throat's muscles. There must be a word for it, she was sure of that, and when she went to the library she looked it up. Phagophobia or anginophobia. She was astonished at the possible phobias. Fear of celestial space and stars. Fear of self and solitude. Rain, crowds, night, ghosts, rivers, feathers, riding trains, heat or hell. And more. Any one of those might be easier to live with than the fear of choking. She finally owned up to it when she realized that she avoided eating when Colin was at work. She tried, but she never managed more than a few bites. He would save her, surely he would, but if she were alone and choked, would she be able to make her way to the nearest neighbor—Lucy—for help?

Colin was allowed to keep his wildness—he hunted and fished. There is a feeling in the early morning, getting up before four to go out into the night while others are sleeping—you're doing what's virtuous and yet, it's a primitive thrill. You'll see what few others do: a white owl on a crooked fence, the spectacle of sunrise. And if he were lucky, he'd kill something. Slit the throat of something. Colin had that. Her wildness was supposed to be plowed under, like a crop you plant to enrich your soil. Her wildness was allowed to come out in bed with him. Let's try this. And this. Ever the inventive lover before they left Ashland, Barbara spent a goodly portion of each day imagining games Colin and she might play abed. Once Colin had said, teasingly, "I hope you'll quit your job someday. It's good for a marriage for the wife to stay home. You'll have time to fantasize." She had laughed. She hadn't been the least bit settled in the job at her parents' gallery. It was something to do until something better came along.

She told Lucy they weren't having sex and Lucy said, "Celibacy and marriage go hand in hand."

"Don't say that—"

"Seduce him." Lucy giggled. "You have to seduce him."

Barbara did not say, I've tried, but she had tried. The timing never seemed right; they were on different cycles of turn-on.

Barbara and Lucy were lying on a slab of granite that jutted into the lake. Ragged yellow aspen leaves shimmered in the autumn wind. Lucy wore a raisin-brown turtleneck and Barbara was tucked into a sleeping bag—it was that cool. The melding of the Southern Comfort and the Amaretto made all things silky, sunladen; every time Lucy moved a fraction, her hair and arms and fingers trailed gold dust.

"I was only fifteen," Lucy said, re-telling, embellishing, the story of falling in love. "In the summer the road crew was sent to repair my mother's road. He was out there, slaving away. All greasy and blackened. Reeking of asphalt. 'I Wanna Hold Your Hand' screamin' from the eight-track. I'd wheel my bike out the lane to go to work. I had a summer job at the café at the Esso. I could feel them all watching me. I thought I was something, oh Jesus yes, I thought that. When you're fifteen you don't know what's in store for you if men think you're good-looking. In a place like this. Finally, he called up one night and I was so stupid. I thought because *he* wanted *me* that meant something. We started going out and I never had a chance after that. He snagged me." She was quiet for a half-minute, smoking, an elegant film-noir grip on her wrinkled roll-your-own cigarette, then she growled, at herself. "That's not the truth. Not all of it."

"Well?"

"You wouldn't believe how I fussed, how I primped, getting dressed to go work at that old café just because I knew he was out there and he'd see me. I snagged him is how he probably sees it. But I never even went out with another boy."

"And you wish you had."

"Of *course*." She stared away from Barbara, toward the lake, leaning back on her elbows, like an organic intrusion, like a part of the rock. "I fell for him hard. At least I know what that feels like. I was crazy about him. And he was crazy about me."

Lucy sipped from the thermos and handed it to her; sipping was all Barbara was capable of. She let the burn of the liquor coat her mouth before she swallowed. She often sat up straight to swallow, in a certain position that made it easier, her head tipped forward. She hoped no one noticed.

She tried on the phrase: crazy about me. Then she turned away from it, as if she'd gotten too close to a red-hot cast-iron eye on a woodstove. Limerence, it was called. She'd read a book about it. It usually lasted two years, and in some cases, created a state of grace that bound couples together after it faded. That was part of the trouble, as Barbara saw it. Colin was never crazy about her. And now she wonders, Was I crazy about him? She must have been, but why? No matter what happens, where you move, who you move in with, what jobs you take and quit, what physical ailments creep up on you, tax problems you have, luck that falls in your lap, you still try, once in a while, to figure out what went wrong.

Lucy sat up and grabbed her fanny pack. With so much anger in those rough hands. She unzipped it jerkily, her head hanging, pose of tears. She wiped at her eyes with the sleeve of her sweater, but soon found a packet of tissues. She cried full force then, she bellowed, and the tissues as she let them go tumbled willy-nilly around the slab of granite and into the lake.

Barbara was afraid to touch her. She waited it out.

"That's why they belly dance," Lucy finally said. "The same thing happened to most of them. They didn't have a chance to live before they got married and had kids. It's socially acceptable to belly dance. You've got to get attention *somewhere*." She looked at her watch. "Cartoons're over and Isaac and Mom are wondering where I am."

"So, why don't you belly dance?"

"I've been thinking about it."

"Seriously?"

"They have competitions. One-shot weekend classes. It'd give us a chance to get away. Matt'd have to watch the kids."

This was the custom. The men watched the children, fed them pizza and sodas and let housekeeping go to hell in a handbasket, while the women went belly dancing. Barbara pictured Colin caring for a child they might have. He would do it willingly and do it well. He would teach a child to recognize trees by their bark and to find springs for drinking water. He would scorn Disney. He would say when to keep your safety on. When they could afford it. Emotionally, she thought. When I can afford it emotionally.

"I'll think about it," Barbara said, indifferently. "I might just go along and take pictures."

"You're not going to stay with him forever."

"Don't say that. This's my last chance."

Colin's face was like an ingot that night over the supper table. A frown squeezed out any good will she might have imagined there. His mind was filled, she presumed, with cylinder heads and wrenches. She had baked a cherry pie that morning. She had hoped the pie would charm him, or that it would lead to a seductive overture, but now it was simply a hedge against any upset.

She wanted to talk, to make up for having talk, talk, talked all afternoon with Lucy, but Colin's surliness flooded the moment. Between small morsels, she tapped her plate with the tines of her fork. Finally, he wadded up his napkin and shoved back from the table. His chair bumped against the bookcase dividing the dining nook from the kitchen area, as if the cabin's dimensions denied him the full expression of his anger.

"What's up?" she said.

He squirmed, still frowning. He shrugged.

"Are you all right?"

"I'm getting sick of it," he said.

"Of what?"

"The job."

Then it all came out. Rescuing big rigs was interesting,

challenging, at first, but now it was boring. He didn't like the men he worked with. His life was drudgery and mind-numbing routine.

There was a barn they passed when driving home from a nearby town. You came upon it by surprise. It was painted bright white and a brick red sign in Old English lettering announced *Hand Weaving & Spinning*. Beyond the barn was the tidy house, with two varnished Dutch doors, and the placid sheep. The woman who lived there had been in business for over twenty years, Lucy had said. She was a community fixture, thriving. Whenever they passed that barn Barbara always had the unsettling feeling that she wasn't long for Echo. That they weren't going to stay. Forces would conspire against them. And this was the start.

"I'm not certain I want to stick with it," Colin said.

Her mouth fell open. "We moved here. It was an enormous hassle." Every word laced with spite. What she meant by that was, *Why is everything about you?*

"I don't need you to tell me that." And then, "You know, you can be a real bitch." He got up and slammed out the door, whistling right away for Gandalf who often went along on his walks. She peeked out the window and watched him bending companionably toward the dog, murmuring to him. She was jealous of the dog.

What if the limerence she felt had been toward Colin rather than Lucy? What if she and Colin had made love the night before and, swimming in that post-coital reservoir of goodwill, he had spoken less harshly and she had been more restrained in her response? Limerence, her therapist tells her, is chemical. Or like weather. It comes and it goes.

The smell of the meat as it congealed was fatty, a smell to make her gag. She threw open the windows. "I'm sick of you," she said out loud, black-heartedly, but not so he could hear. "Sick."

Delighted that they wanted to belly dance, Mavis said, "Come along to Kamloops next weekend. It's a workshop—for all levels. I can lend you outfits." They went to her house to pick them out. She had to show off the spacious log house—the vacuum built into the wall—and then serve them tea with scones and clotted cream. In pleated skirts and knee-highs, her twin girls—around grade five, Barbara guessed—sat cross-legged before the television, chewing gum, their necks cricked up to a soap opera. It was the late afternoon, the hour of Sicilian Kisses, such ambrosial betrayal, and the contrast between tea with Mavis and the acute intimacy of drinking with Lucy beside the lake gave Barbara pause. Nibbling at the scone, she saw too clearly how far she had strayed from her original intention. All those good intentions unrealized, the road to hell, her mother would've reminded her.

Mavis took them into the bedroom where she had laid out costumes pieces on the bed. Bras crusted with bangles and beads, scarves, beaded belts. All spangly, garish, over the top. Not the least bit sexy, in Barbara's opinion.

Mavis assured them primly, "It's not a sexual thing, you know. Belly dancing is a family activity. People have funny ideas about it, but you just need to explain."

That night, in a conciliatory manner, Colin said, "So try it on for me, would you?" He had built a fire in the little Airtight. The stovepipe glowed. Outside, switches and limbs brushed against the windows. A damp wind had stripped the leaves from the trees; the best of fall was over, the golden days.

Barbara squirmed. "I'd rather not. I'm not even sure I'll do it."

His face fell and went blank. He turned on the television, to their one station, and pretended to care about the news program just ending on the snowy screen.

Barbara tried to remember when they had last made love. It had to have been nearly two months before; they had christened the cabin two or three times to establish their territory. But since then, the evenings had been spent reading or writing letters, with the quiet encroaching. Twice they had driven to Kamloops for a movie. Colin often went to bed early. She often stayed up late. When she went to bed in the dark, she would feel with her fingertips the logs of the bedroom wall, trying not to wake him. The walls felt like nothing she ever imagined she would live with. The word shabby came to mind. Her mother would die if she knew. Later in the winter her mother would come for a visit. She would cry on the little deck when she saw how they were living and how much weight Barbara had lost. Barbara would ask to go home with her, but her mother would say, "You'll regret it. Stick it out."

If only she were allowed to look for a job, but her immigration papers did not permit her to work until later, the next year. She would apply to clerk at the camera shop in town. Or she might be a substitute teacher. She wanted to be able to say that to her parents—I'm looking for a job. Her father had always stressed the importance of work. She had complained about the gallery—its silence, its pretension—but she missed it now.

With Colin breathing sleepily beside her, she would think of her mother and father in Ashland, the green shows, the gallery, with its wine-and-cheese openings, wearing a little black dress and a string of pearls like a costume, speaking of Gustave Baumann or Impressionism as familiars, and she would knead her private sorrow. She would ask, What have I done with the only life I have? What an idiot, she'd think. And then she would hear her mother's voice, admonishing, fearful, "Don't call yourself that." Never say that. Never, never. Her father would throw up his hands after a bad business decision came home to roost or after he'd had a fender bender, which happened more than once or twice, and he'd call himself Stupid! Idiot! She had picked up the habit from him.

The trip to Kamloops involved a caravan of cars, nineteen women and their costumes and overnight gear. Hilarity burst like thunder every few minutes in each car. Barbara and Lucy had hopped into the backseat of the Spanish teacher's car, determined to be together. The Spanish teacher was the oldest among the belly dancers; single; amply built, almost brutish. A nurse from the clinic had taken the passenger seat—Gloria. A sweet thin woman who smoked with them at every rest stop.

It was the weekend before Halloween and there was much talk of the upcoming dance at the community hall, the local band, what people were wearing and what they had worn the year before. The Spanish teacher said she'd gone as a slut. Black slip, no underwear. Gloria had been a Woody-Allen-ish sperm. Barbara had thought that Colin would refuse to go, but out of the blue he had said, "Think I'll be a pirate." He wanted to wear a black moustache and a tri-corner hat. A sword was in the works at the shop. The night before the Kamloops trip he had said, "Why don't you be a belly dancer?" She refused. She wanted to say, I'm not even *going* to the Halloween dance. I hate Halloween. She wanted to stay home and read, but that would be impossible. She would not be able to concentrate, wondering who would dance with whom, what titillating comments might be made when people were wasted. Pissed, her neighbors called it—if you were drunk in Canada, you were pissed.

At the wheel, the Spanish teacher said, "Wouldn't it be wonderful to wear masks so that no one knew who you were? You'd be free to do whatever all night?" She guided the steering wheel with her knee and used both hands to open a bag of malted milk balls. She passed them around.

Gloria said, "Whatever?"

"Guilt-free."

"I'm going to be a gypsy," Barbara said, shaking her head *No* to the malt balls. She could imagine the melting chocolate, the cloying pick-me-up, but her throat closed up at the idea. She wondered where the nearest hospital was and how long a person could survive not breathing before brain damage set in. She had not quit eating entirely, but she had her rules. Always eat at a table or counter, sitting down, with other people present. Take small bites. Sip water after each small bite. She crushed her vitamins and mixed the resultant powder up with honey. And so on. "Gypsies're commonplace, but I have the wig for it." She pictured the wig, soot black and swirly with curls, stored under the bed in a box of photography props she had used with children—fake noses and eyebrows, shawls and canes and old-time hats.

Lucy smiled her secret smile. "Tell fortunes, why don't you?"

Gloria told a story of having her tarot cards read. It went on for a while. She left no card unturned. It was a story of irreparable mistakes, love gone wrong, mirrors blackened, and moves that allowed her to become a new person, sort of, by coming home to

Echo. At the end of the story, she said, "We have to tell secrets tonight, don't we?"

The Spanish teacher said, "How else would we amuse ourselves?"

Lucy gave Barbara that slit-eyed glance, as if to say, "Will we? Tell secrets?"

What no one knew was that Barbara had still not made up her mind to belly dance. They raved about the teacher, said she was fabulous, very nurturing.

The workshop was to be held in a YWCA next to a steakhouse. They checked in to the resort across the street from the Y, four to a room. The resort was built on cliffs above a river; she didn't know the name of the river and wondered why she had made so little effort to learn the names of rivers, streams, mountains. Lucy and she threw down their duffle bags on the same queen bed, and Lucy went into the bathroom. That was Barbara's chance: she grabbed her sweatshirt and purse.

Outdoors the sky and trees had the washed-out feel of fall past its prime. All color faded. It wasn't quite Halloween. Winter would come soon and with it months of auto-follies, scooching under the truck to put on chains, dead batteries, sliding off the icy road into ditches. Still, right then the river was a beautiful navy blue. She didn't have a car; she would have to appreciate whatever caught her eye within walking distance. On the hills and tawny benches of land, orchards rolled away in several directions. At the nearest one, pickers charged up and down ladders, canvas bags strapped on, the bags full of apples. Tractors hauling wooden bins chugged up and down the rows in blossoms of diesel exhaust. Down below the cliff she could see kayakers, a covey of them, playing in a big wave. They weren't headed anywhere, on a mission, not proving anything. They were only playing. She sat down on a rock to watch. Their boats were purple and green and hot pink, like shuttles weaving joy of the water. She was relieved not to be belly dancing in a scratchy sequined bra. She missed water and swimming, missed it fiercely, and had brought her suit—a reflex while packing—and now knew why.

Her worn-thin bathing suit was white with a black stripe

around the waist, baggy on her, and that might be a problem—how much weight she had lost—but it didn't matter. Not right then.

She spent the afternoon in the Y pool. There were two lanes for lap swimmers and she swam for a half-hour, rested, and swam again. How luxurious it felt to float, to shed the burden of her body. She talked to the lifeguard, a jolly teenage girl with a luscious rind of swimmer's fat on her thighs and arms. She watched small slight children in goggles, taking lessons; they were so serious about breathing, so serious about shivering, with towels wrapped around their shoulders. The light and water undulated on the walls like seaweed. And late in the afternoon, she joined in the aerobics class with nine plump women in Speedo suits. John Cougar blasted from the teacher's stereo, humdrum stories of lust and disappointment.

At the evening meal, no one said anything about her absence. Only Mavis cast a silent question her way. Barbara shrugged. Smiled. Swimming had made her feel reborn.

The women were all full of themselves, more fully themselves, loose-limbed, noisy, laughing, pleading, joking, flirting with the waiter, a sandy-haired man with a farmboy's guile-free grin and muscles. You could imagine him bucking bales. They consumed large quantities of Australian red wine and licked chocolate mousse from their lips. Lucy seemed happy, relaxed around the eyes, in a green sweater that fit her perfectly. She leaned over and whispered, "I hope you weren't bored."

"No way," Barbara said. "I needed to be alone." She was able to eat, wild rice—no chicken—broccoli florets, tomato wedges, rolls and butter. She ate with only a shim of doubt about whether she could swallow. It was the first meal in weeks she had eaten with gusto.

Later, they piled into one large room, a pajama party, with the radio station playing Sam Cooke. A case of wine had been pulled miraculously from someone's car. It was Sam Cooke Night and they listened to "You Send Me" and "You're Nobody 'Till Somebody Loves You" and "Try a Little Love." The disc jockey had a radio voice that was positively orgasmic, Mavis said, and the disc jockey intoned, "Sam Cooke's vision never ceased to grow." In that soul beat, that mercy, women massaged each other's shoulders and backs and thighs and calves, leaning into each other, pairing off for a tete-a-tete, patting each other's cheeks or shoulders, weeping now and then, howling with laughter, then sighing, standing with a whimper—how sore they were—pouring more wine, observing the fray and deciding where to join in again. The lights were dim, the air perfumy. Out the sliding glass door, beyond the balcony, was the reality of river and night, husbands, children, emergency rooms, weedy gardens, cats with pinkeye, dog fights, trash cans raccoons had upturned, broken appliances, science projects that failed, nightmares, stretch marks, sheets that needed changing, checks that bounced, cakes that fell, milk spilled, tomahawk throws, courses they signed up for and had to quit, the vulture wings of time hovering. They would never be this young again. They felt it and said so. Moaning at the unfairness. The rudeness of it.

Gloria came into the room in a gray flannel robe, her hair damp, her face shiny. She wended her way to the sliding glass door and held up a pack of Players. "Smoke?"

Barbara went out to the balcony with her. It was cool, breezy. She pulled up the hood of her sweatshirt. Domestic lights glimmered all along the lakeshore. Gloria lit a cigarette and flipped it around, offering it to Barbara. She lit one for herself and they smoked for a moment in silence. Then Gloria squeaked, "I love these women. Even Mavis."

Barbara laughed. Even Mavis. She felt included in the prevalent criticism of Mavis, without another word being spoken.

She could see her camera on the nightstand, the lens cover dangling by a thin black cord. At the ready. The women had agreed that she should document the night. She had taken a few posed shots, women with their temples together, cheeks brushing, smiling for the camera. But the ruckus had gotten out of hand; emotional; private; unpredictable. She felt like an intruder.

"Soon they'll start the secrets."

"Should I be nervous?" Barbara said.

"No pressure," Gloria said.

Two boys walked by dribbling a basketball, ga-bang, ga-bang, ga-bang. On another balcony, a man in a ruffled tuxedo shirt popped open a bottle of champagne. Smoke from woodstoves tainted the air, cozily.

Barbara's head felt a little wine-woozy and she said, "When you move, every thought is a secret. Until you make friends."

"I've never wanted to be far from Echo," Gloria said. She talked about her husband then, the principal of the elementary school. He was kind, he knew how to hang drywall and repair faucets, he gave dynamite backrubs, he read to the kids at night. She had no complaints about him.

Barbara watched Gloria, leaning like a sprite into the wind, her hands pressing on the balcony rail. Without make-up, her features seemed blurred. She thought, Will we be friends? The chemistry didn't seem to be there. Lucy had spoiled her; would she ever have that kind of chemistry again?

Inside, the women in the saffron light turned toward the television in its armoire, and at first, from the balcony, Barbara thought: They're going to watch TV. But that wasn't it. They were settling themselves, wine in hand in plastic motel cups. Mavis went around the room, climbing over women, turning down the lamps. Barbara sought out Lucy, but she didn't spot her. She felt a bit adrift, with Lucy out of view.

And then Lucy stepped out of the bathroom, in a bra and belly dancing belt shimmering with copper beads. Tendrils of silver scarves curled around her legs. She looked athletic, sure-footed. Mavis consulted with her over music—this tape? Or this? Mavis popped a tape into the black recorder on top of the television: jazz, serpentine saxophone. On the balcony Barbara and Gloria heard the music as if from underwater.

Lucy went back into the bathroom, scarves switching, and closed the door. Someone chirped, "No stalling!" After ten seconds more, Lucy made her entrance. She was the main event. For me, Barbara thought. She's been the main event.

"Looks like her fantasy," Gloria whispered. "A stripper. She's a stripper."

Strip tease. The words had never had much meaning to Barbara before. Lucy took her time. She reveled in it. When finally she unclasped her bra, there was a visible sigh among the women; Lucy's breasts were still wondrous, in spite of iridescent stretch marks. One by one, she tugged off the scarves that made up her skirt, tossing them in the air, and then the beaded belt. It all took time. Barbara's hands trembled from the cold and desire.

If only she could reach her camera. Possess the moment. If only, if only. Lucy wore lace panties and rolled them, inch by inch, over her hips and down until they wavered from the toes of one raised foot, the poppy red toenails seeming to flirt from within the lace. The music on the homemade tape cut to big band horns, the spell broken.

The women applauded, a wild spanking. Lucy stood before them, naked, flushed, proud.

Barbara's heart was laid low with honesty: she glimpsed her own predatory urges. How ruled she'd been by that. All those afternoons at the lake, all that liquor, addictive truth-telling. It had been about wanting Lucy as Matt did. Later she wrapped up in a foam-like motel blanket; she slept on the floor, not trusting herself to lie beside Lucy without saying what was stuck in her throat.

Halloween evening, Barbara dressed in a peasant blouse embroidered with forget-me-knots, a long broomstick skirt, the black wig and make-up to match: carmine lipstick and nails, sooty eyes. She had borrowed a tambourine, and devised a fortune-telling ball from a security light bulb swaddled in purple velvet in a tobacco tin. She did not recognize herself. Her mind's eye kept flashing to an image of a painting of a gypsy woman by a Barcelona painter— she could not remember his name. The woman's beauty was plain; her cheeks were the terra cotta of the wall behind her. But Halloween was not about beauty or truth, and she wanted that to be all right, permissible, with the part of herself who remembered the gypsy woman. She wanted to let go of those images from the gallery. She wound a string of brass coins in her hair.

Her eating had been better all week. Every day she had remembered the pool, the wavering light on the walls, the immersive delight. She could drive there any time she needed to. It was a long drive for a swim, but she had to do what mattered. When she thought of the pool, she could swallow food or drink with only remnants of fear, not her former anxiety, the full-blown emergency.

And Lucy—Lucy had no idea what kept her from coming over to visit. She would never tell. Years later, this would be the worst regret, what still brought tears to her eyes: that she never told Lucy. She cannot call up Lucy and say, Remember when? She has perused the Echo website and she recognizes the names of the Town Council members and the volunteer fire chief, the weaver, the woman who ran the dairy where they bought their raw milk in half-gallon jars. But there is no Lucy Givens.

Colin came in from work, tossing his empty lunch box on the sofa.

Later, in the crystalline winter, he would lose his job. They would sell Christmas trees to make money for food. Her father would die of an abdominal aneurysm and her mother would cry on the deck. They would have decisions to make. Vagaries, difficulties, lay ahead. They were too young to anticipate that, although she would mark this night, Halloween in the cabin in Echo, British Columbia, as the night she knew something was wrong with them that might not be repaired.

He took a beer from the refrigerator and turned on the television; she heard all this and waited until it sounded as if he were settled. She shimmied gypsy-like out into the living room, thrummed the tambourine, and said, "Ta-da!" Colin was hunched toward the round mirror beside the front door, trying on his pirate moustache. He turned to her, his face lit up.

Sheepishly, as if he'd almost forgotten how to express want, he came over and lifted her breasts, squeezing too hard. "You look so different," he said, sounding glad.

"Not yet," she said.

"Come on, Barb—"

"Let's wait till after. I'm all ready to go—"

He nudged her back into the bedroom. She heard the scrabble of mice nesting in the gutters, wanting in from the cold.

"Wait, wait," she said. "Let's wait till *after*. I'm ready to go."

But Colin acted as if he hadn't heard. She tried to evade him, to twist away, but the room was tiny and he was strong. She thought, All right. It's what I've wanted. It wasn't as if they had an aversion to quickies. They had been on the same wavelength then, in the apartment in Ashland, with the Shakespeare Festival banners whipping in the wind outside. Afterwards, they would laugh at their lust, its intensity.

She wanted to reach out and say, Come to me, to the same wavelength. Touch my hand. Tell me a secret. How long had it been since she had touched his hand?

He unzipped his pants and flung her down on the bed, his fake pirate moustache gleaming above her. "It's all that hair," he whispered hoarsely. He expertly got rid of whatever cloth lay between them. He fucked someone she wasn't, someone she could never be.

OTHER HEARTBREAKS

Skylark

Emma Compartmentalizes in Ireland

Ephemera

SKYLARK

"WOW," HIS SON-IN-LAW LUIS SAID when he first saw the Skylark. "Looks like a sports car on steroids."

Joe loves the original factory paint job—Pinehurst Green Metallic, sage in some lights, turquoise in others—and the horn button engraved with his father's name: Customized for Robert March. He loves the white convertible top, the Kelsey-Hayes wire wheels and the whitewall tires, the chunky chrome grill, the satisfying muted thwack when he closes the door. He loves the way heads turn when he maneuvers it down the street. He thinks of it as a public service; people get a kick out of vintage cars.

A Saturday, St. Patrick's Day, at the wheel Joe watches the door for Emma's bright blue beret. He thinks that she's in there with Sophie, last-minute mother-daughter whatever. He has learned from his daughters how to say *whatever*. Are they plotting against him? Emma wants to move to the north side, to be near her school in the decade remaining until she retires. To keep himself in the present—Emma's #1 dictum—he contemplates his inventory, a little like a king in his counting house.

Near 18th and Ashland Ave, heart of the Mexicano port of entry, Home Plate must be sought out. "It's true," his father used to say, "it doesn't jump out and bite you on the ass. But, Joey, it's better that way. You got your serious collectors." They come to purchase and weasel and barter and bargain: bleacher seats, jerseys, cleats, tickets from famous games, signed balls, what have you, mostly American flotsam, what washes up on Joe's step. What washed up on his father's step before Joe took over. And what he keeps in a safe deposit box at LaSalle Bank, his nest egg, foundation of his sketchy retirement plan: a signed Ty Cobb card, Babe Ruth's key to San Francisco, and a signed photo of Marilyn Monroe at bat in white short-shorts.

Joe likes to say he's the last of the bohunks in Pilsen, and a half-blood at that. His mother's family came to Chicago from Bohemia, his father's family from Liverpool, small-time merchants and repairmen. Practical people. His father started out as a bicycle repairman and worked his way up to management at Schwinn. He ended his days at Home Plate, slumped over the counter from a massive heart attack. When Joe thinks of dying, he imagines cremation—the church allows that now. Until 9/11 he wanted his ashes scattered in his own tomato patch behind the shop. He had hoped a neighbor woman from La Paz or Guadalajara might make salsa from his bohunk ashes.

Vapor-thin fog curls around the corner, where a tamale cart steams in front of San Pio, the vendor waiting for the post-Mass Saturday morning faithful. If only Emma would hurry and keep him company, keep him from his memories. That seems to be one of the big differences between being his age—almost seventy—and being Emma's age, not quite fifty-five: he lives in memory.

For Joe March, good memories are the worst. Love and surprise. Yes, youth. A time before regret. The life everlasting, as his old friend Gerald Stern wrote. Vivaldi years. He thinks of Stern as his old friend, but he doesn't know him. Not personally. He keeps his poetry books beside the bed. He likes the jacket photo on *The Red Coal:* young Gerald Stern and Jack Gilbert in Paris, maybe returning from a brothel. A spring in their steps.

Today the Skylark reminds Joe of Sylvia, his only Jewish girlfriend. If Emma comes out, Sylvia will fade and he might keep even keel. Sylvia's family disapproved. He called her "Sunshine," a bold move, he thought at the time, giving a girl a nickname.

It was 1953, he was sixteen, the Rosenbergs had just been executed. His brother was still alive, but he died a few years later from a blood disease. Even after fifty-odd years, the anniversary of his brother's death lies in ambush at the start of April.

At last Emma emerges and Joe gets out and with a magnanimity he has to fake he opens the passenger door. The CLOSED sign has not been flipped. Sophie promised to cover for him, so where

is she? Joe grudgingly wonders if she'll slap up a beefcake photo
of Mike Piazza in the window. His girls are ruled by hormones,
and it's all out in the open, no subtlety. Sophie married, but running around the house in an orange slip with lace trim that doesn't
cover her up top. Liz, a flight attendant, until recently trolling on
the job, guy to guy, men she didn't bother to introduce to them.
Now she's moved in with one. He gets the lowdown from Emma.

He waves to Emma, little kid wave with his fingers, still faking, on the way around the hood to the driver's side. Crowds funnel
along the sidewalk now, flea market-goers on their way to Canal-
port, and children running, tagging each other, teasing, and loiter-
ers, adolescents who hang—that's the expression, Joe's been told.
Glassine envelopes are traded for wrinkled cash. Once he asked
Luis, "What goes on out there?" And Luis said, "Wraps. In-di-vi-
dual portions of crack. And other substances. They're in a world of
hurt." He punctuated the air with his thumb and forefinger circled,
like a chef discussing a special. Luis works for Ceasefire, a network bent on ending street violence. When someone dies he goes
to the hospital and in the blood and bone of the emergency room,
he persuades the perpetrators to break the chain. Every time he
rushes out, Joe wants to haul him back inside and bolt the door.

The car floats away from the curb and Emma slides in a CD.
She removes her beret, which is too bad—he likes the maverick
look of it; she pats it onto the back seat next to a pastry box of
zeppoles, left there by Uncle Leo in anticipation of Joe's feast day,
Monday. It's long been tradition in his family to avoid St. Patrick's
Day and celebrate St. Joseph's feast day. He's studied enough history to know that the Irish in charge of Chicago treated the Bohemians and Italians hard when they first arrived in the new world.
Tit for tat. The Bohemians and Italians rejected Saint Paddy. Joe is
glad to be getting out of town.

He says, "I wish Uncle Leo wouldn't tempt me like that."

Emma says, "I think the ordinary, family rituals make him
feel better. He's in dire straits."

Dire straits: Uncle Leo—nearly ninety, a retired Dominican
friar, old enough to know better—is up on criminal charges, plain
and simple. He and a wild-eyed Jesuit took a sledgehammer to a

fighter jet at Grissom Air Force Base. Civil disobedience in the extreme.

He reaches for Emma's hand. Emma is kind to Uncle Leo and that goes a long way with him. He squeezes her hand. They have not reconnected since breakfast yesterday; Emma was out late, congregating with fellow teachers at a blues bar on the north side. Joe stayed home and watched *Groundhog Day* with his friend and former student Benny, possibly the tenth time they've watched it. It soothes the soul, Benny says.

They take his favorite route, through Chinatown, onto South Lakeshore Drive, with its curves and harbors, the sailboats bobbing in the tarnished winter water. Emma is resting, eyes closed, recovering from the school week. They pass the site in Jackson Park where the Army maintained nuclear warheads to defend Chicago during the Cold War. That would be a plus-feature now: to have warheads at the ready.

Once they leave Jackson Park and begin the tricky part, the trek down Jeffrey Boulevard, Emma opens her eyes and helps him drive, which to her means scanning, daring someone to jerk out from a parking spot or run a red light. But Joe takes it slow.

A concerned Emma says, "How're your eyes?"

"Don't bug me, Emma." Beginning cataracts and macular degeneration—there's never anything to say about that sort of gradual wearing away of what was, until recently, a fully functioning bell or whistle. He still has a full head of hair, white as sugar, and for that he is grateful. "Sorry, sweets."

"I accept your apology." Emma reaches for a road atlas; she opens Montana wide on her lap. Her travel fantasies irk him.

"You missed Dom Silva last night." As soon as the words are out of his mouth, he regrets it.

"What did Dom Silva have to say for himself?"

"What he always says. I'm not selling. The house is for Luis and Sophie."

Long pause. Long pause in which—he can tell—Emma tries to decide how far to push it. One of their habitual conflicts is about to rise up, many-headed beast. Next, she'd be asking, Why can't you move the shop to Wrigleyville? If I have to keep teaching, I want to be able to walk to school. By that she would mean, if you can't support us, I want a major concession. Why in the world did your father think he could make a living off the beaten path? This was all part and parcel of her domestic campaign to move out of Pilsen, where they have lived for twenty-seven years, convenient to the Blue Line. His heart lub-lubs; how is it his heart beats along like a champ without him noticing unless he's pissed? Then he feels it pounding and worries it might stop.

Emma says, "Luis and Sophie don't even want it."

"We used to agree on that."

They pass Chicago Vocational High School, bleak citadel, home of the Cavaliers, their school colors navy blue and gold, a fact Joe seems to have squirreled away when Alonzo Redding pitched for CVHS before he was picked up by the Winston-Salem Warthogs. This train of thought, the minor leagues, spring training, the aperture a game gives, a place to test your lungs—all that makes his irritation not worth a tinker's damn.

Once on the toll road, Emma reaches for *his* hand and squeezes it, Morse code for, if not apology, the illusion of apology. As if she has divined his thoughts.

He squeezes back.

All the way through East Chicago and Gary, the Rust Belt, the industrial maze laid out before them stirs Joe, the ports and shipping containers and fuel tanks and smoke stacks a little like the thrill of a patriotic pre-movie newsreel he looked forward to in the fifties. He takes the chance of giving Emma a history lesson, what he's fairly sure she already knows. After all, she teaches 7th grade. (That thought is always followed by this one: she's the primary breadwinner. Not a phrase Joe would use, but ever since Emma said it, he can't get it out of his head.)

"In the 1800's the Potowatamis lived in villages—fifty villages—around the tip of Lake Michigan. One hundred years later, Judge Gary's dream of a gigantic steel mill was a reality and the city of Gary became the—"

"Wasteland of America," Emma says.

He has heard that the EPA refers to the area as a National Sacrifice Zone. He says, "No one knew what to expect. People were innocent then. Now you can't buy a candy bar without feeling guilty about the wrapper."

Kind of Blue ends.

Emma says, "Did you hear anything about that girl?"

"She's still in critical condition at RUSH. Twelve years old."

"Jesus, Joe—"

Joe sighs, sorry to have to tell her. Every time a child is shot, he thinks, How the hell can this happen again? And then he forgets until the next time, the forgetting reminiscent of the way he categorizes terrorist acts. He doesn't want to read the long accounts of terrorism in the newspaper. All those tourists killed in Egypt in 1996. The USS Cole. The churches bombed in Indonesia. He still thinks of them as isolated incidents.

"Don't start."

"I'm not *starting*. I'm way past starting."

Joe bites his tongue to keep from wrangling; he can't talk about moving, not today. He counts to ten and turns on the radio. "How about a little music? A little soundtrack?" He searches for a station, settling for something rosy, classical.

"I'm sorry," Emma offers. "Sorry we're not getting along. I must be cranky. I'm concerned about Liz." She grabs a pillow from the back seat, tucks it against the door, sighs into it, and closes her eyes.

On I-94, in the six-lanes of traffic beclouded with exhaust, mostly bellicose semis, Joe misses her. He ventures, "Is there anything I can do? For Liz?" Their older daughter has recently taken up with a man with a child—a twelve-year-old boy. Nothing wrong with that exactly, Joe tells himself, but he worries about her. He has a hard time imagining his girls grown up. He wants them safely back in the shop, doing their homework, while he sorts baseball cards. He wants to roll back time.

Emma naps on.

One hour later the stressful driving is over and they're on a straight-away two-lane blacktop, with the occasional dazzle of crocuses,

Jersey milk cows in a field, suddenly pastoral. He's almost forgotten where they're going. That Uncle Mort, his mother's brother, bequeathed them his ten organic acres.

Joe says, "Haven't we been a good example to the girls? As a couple?"

"I think so." She gives him her best smile and a bright-eyed glance. "Look. It's like that David Hockney painting—you know— the road through patchwork fields."

"It's spring over here." She *thinks* so. Goddamn lukewarm answer if there ever was one. But the irritation of the morning is gone and Joe anticipates complicity with the realtor, a chipper woman he's spoken with by phone several times, and he anticipates a hearty lunch—maybe they can find one of those Italian places where the two of them can eat for sixteen dollars and someone in the family makes the sauce from scratch—and then the trip back. The sun might come out. They cross a creek and pass blueberry farms, the blueberry shrubs not yet in leaf.

"Is this our turn?" Emma says, a good navigator, lover of maps.

They turn down a road more serpentine than the last, and tucked here and there among the hills and dales are new, big, expensive homes in various stages of completion, raw plywood still visible, the yards tumbled with soil, not yet landscaped.

Joe muses, "Mort would've been only three or four when they left the old country. After he grew up, he worked at a catsup factory in Marion. When they laid him off he moved up here. City life—he didn't have much use for it."

He slows to a crawl, watching for a landmark, a clue. The last time he visited Uncle Mort was nearly fifty years ago.

"How much do you think these lots are going for?"

"Plenty," Joe says, then, "This is it. See those hemlocks—"

He creeps into a driveway with a grassy hump down the middle and chipped gravel, pulverized, in the tire tracks. Emma has to crane her neck to see the tops of the hemlocks. She says, "We have that in common, Joe."

"What's that?"

"The love of names, specifics. We might need a guidebook to trees."

He knows her well enough to know that she's envisioning their summer trip.

"Earth to Emma," he says.

"I'm right here."

More hemlocks, with their drooping crowns, line the driveway plunging deep into the property, a long narrow trapezoid according to their copy of the appraisal. A small barn, once red, now gray, kneels into the ground, with its splintered Dutch doors flung open and moss growing on the north slant of roof. A dead rooster lies in the chicken yard, inside a sagging wire fence.

Emma says, "This might be hard. But it won't take long. I hope."

The house is white clapboard, two-story, with tall windows and a frosted glass front door. A wide veranda fronts the house. Joe parks and squints up. Black squirrels dart up a tree, fussing. "Black squirrels. That's a new one on me." He peers out the windshield. "Let's take a look around."

"But my shoes."

Why didn't she wear sturdy shoes? She's wearing black leather slippers. She didn't prepare for the country. For mud and gravel. Dead chickens.

Emma checks her watch. "What time is she coming?"

"Noon."

"It's noon now."

"She'll be here any minute." Then: "You love the great outdoors."

"I love walks. Not farms."

"I want to get out and look around. I was here two or three times. I came here once for a week. I'd forgotten that. Come on, sweets—get out with me."

She already has her beret on again; curiosity won't let her sit in the car. She'll have an adventure for her students on Monday. Joe goes around and opens Emma's door. She delicately places her shoes on chosen dry spots and he takes her elbow and tips her up and out of the Skylark. Emma leans into him, kisses his cheek.

"That's nice," Joe says.

He holds her hand and navigates the muddy yard, around to the first gardens. The gardens go on acres beyond. They enter one plot demarcated by stones and a wire fence. Joe kneels and carefully tears away damp straw, down to the soil, and he smiles up at her and says, "Look—a strawberry patch. There's new growth already."

"I need a bathroom, Joe."

"Let's check out the inside."

The back screen door hangs from one hinge. "It's too much," Emma says, indicating the trash barrels on the screened back porch, filled with batches of beer brewing, the yeasty odor, the empty brown bottles, the rusty chest freezer, a bathtub, the slippery pile of damp, yellowing magazines and newspapers—*Soviet Life* from 1957 is the one on top. Spiders inhabit empty canning jars. The walls are plastered with calendars—seed calendars and girlie motorcycle calendars from thirty years ago.

"How did he get away with living like this?"

"He's off the main road."

She pries open the next door. In the kitchen, linoleum peels from the floor. A mouse or mole scratches underfoot. She reaches for his hand, but she doesn't squeal—he gives her credit for that. At Emma's school, there are mice and snakes and she handles them with equanimity.

He opens the door to a closet-size bathroom with an avocado green commode and basin, an aluminum box shower. The tie-dyed psychedelic shower curtain is streaked with mold. A photo of Fidel Castro in his prime is tacked on the wall directly in front of the toilet.

The shut bathroom door muffling her voice, Emma says, "It's the land they'll want. In the summer this house'll be razed. Some poor soul'll have the imagination for it. The trees are a selling point. The trees and the gardens. By that time, you and I will be hiking. In the Alps."

You can't blame a man or woman for having dreams; Joe recalls a National Geographic Special, the latest scientific evidence, purporting that our dreams and desires are one more biological imperative. The woman in a white lab coat on the program said that people differ in the degree to which they seek stimulation. But the most enduring couples—no surprise there—are those whose natural levels of sensation-seeking, whether high, low, or in-between, are closely aligned. High sensation-seekers chase novelty and their dopamine levels increase and they get an all-around rush they associate with their partners. Hence Emma's dream of traveling in Europe with him. Of resuscitating who they were when they fell in love. Teachers at the boarding school in Locarno. If only her novelty were his.

Joe returns to the strawberry patch, and she finds him on his knees, mud wicking into the denim of his jeans. Sunshine cuts through the clouds in sharp pillars. He says, "My mother and I visited Uncle Mort for that week."

"I thought they weren't close."

"Not usually. There was that one visit. Right after the war." Meaning World War Two, he starts to say, but holds his tongue; that might sound patronizing. "He gardened out here without a stitch on and my mother didn't seem to mind. They had something in common. Politics. They were political like Uncle Leo. Mucking about, subversive. I didn't understand what they were talking about. I didn't want to."

"What about your brother?"

"I don't know why he didn't come."

Joe sits down on a wooden stool, a *milking* stool. The diamond in his wedding band catches light. His knuckles are a little misshapen, his hands spotted. "What I liked about being here," Joe goes on, "was the growth. You can't imagine what it's like in summer. He's got fruit trees in a field a little farther back. Apricots were coming in. Not much bigger than his thumb—the sugar was concentrated."

"You have good memories, Joe."

If she only knew. "Do you like it here?"

"I'm a townie, you know me," she says. "I'm going back to the car."

"Suit yourself." He lifts a moldy bundle of straw, sets it aside.

He imagines a box of postcards and letters in a closet, written by his Bohemian kin. Immigrants all, in the early part of the 20th century. The letters had been old when Uncle Mort let him read them all those years ago, old and toast brown along the edges, some of them half-crumpled, or written in pencil like a grocery list, not considered precious. It was their habit to write notes to each other mid-week. They wrote about noodles and headcheese. Gardening details. What time they went to Mass. Gossip they heard from the old country, who had fallen ill, who had married or run off across the border to work in Budapest. Their handwriting was impeccable, unhurried. A stamp for a letter cost two cents. A postcard, a penny. They had simple goals, so far as he could tell. They wanted life to improve on the material plane and they wanted to be good citizens. His mother did all that organizing. She circulated petitions. Wrote letters to the editor. And, when she gained confidence in herself, she gave rousing talks at rallies. According to his brother. For Joe had nothing but indifference for what she did—he never went to a single political event. And now, if only he had the memory of that.

He had been enthralled with Sylvia.

Whatever happened to Sylvia? They kissed a few times. Once she lied to her mother and rode with his family to the dunes on the southeasterly tip of the lake. His father liked to drive to what his mother called the ends of the earth. They would eat salami-on-rye sandwiches with French's mustard. The sandwiches would be slightly sandy. He pictures the Skylark—big boat of a car, sign of plenty—as it was on the asphalt parking lot against the gray beach when he and Sylvia approached it coming back from a walk. He held her hand and their hands were damp together, trembling with ardor. She wept on the way home, ashamed that she had lied to her mother, but only he knew why; his mother sat up front and frowned across the high seatback, wondering what was wrong with their young love. Beside him, his brother stared out the window, embarrassed to be privy to the drama. Sylvia's father bought a T-shirt shop on the boardwalk in Ocean City, Maryland, and that seemed a world away. They wrote a few letters and then didn't. With what happiness he opened those letters.

Joe's father had just purchased the Skylark from a dealer in Evanston—it was June. His mother, Uncle Leo, and his brother went uptown for the prayer vigil the night the Rosenbergs were executed. His brother was fourteen. Over three thousand people gathered at a church that night. A little like the vigils after 9/11. At home, later, his mother's eyes were pink-rimmed, wet. His brother lay on the bottom bunk bed in the room they shared, his arm over his face. Joe and his father were high about the Skylark and they didn't want to think about anything else. Most men are selfish that way. He doesn't want to be that way now. He doesn't think he is.

His father tolerated what she did. He just tolerated it. His father in management at Schwinn resented UAW organizing the bicycle workers. He resented the role UAW played in the demise of Schwinn in Chicago. After that, he retreated to Home Plate. End of the line for him. If Joe's mother would say, "The immigrant story is a political story," he would say, "It's baseball, baseball and other sports, that make an immigrant an American. It's where we come together. Politics—that tears people apart." They both had their points, chronic arguments they refined over time.

Only his aching knees bring him back to the moldy straw in his hand, the bobwhites whistling.

Emma perches on the top veranda step, petting a stray kitten the color of a dingy cloud. Joe stands before her with soiled hands, smiling, coaxingly. He says, "Satchmo would love it here, don't you think?"

"Satchmo's an indoor cat. You know that."

"Oh, Emma."

"We're selling this place."

"I thought you wanted to move."

"Not *here*."

Joe droops down pensively beside her. He pulls a cigar from his shirt pocket and sniffs it. She wants the city. The Art Institute and the galleries. The jazz fest. Joe reaches for her. "Come here, sweets." He's not faking. At last, he's not faking.

"I don't want to come there. Tell me."

Joe rises, tucks his hands in the pockets of his jeans. In a conciliatory whisper, he says, "Damn it, Emma. I don't want to sell yet. I just. *Don't*."

The realtor's white Toyota pickup grinds down the driveway, her metal FOR SALE signs rattling in the bed, some easy listening love song squirting out her rolled down window.

Joe hadn't noticed that Emma has a can of mackerel beside her, a can of mackerel and a rusty spoon. But he smells it, finally. She must've gone in the front door and back to the kitchen and into Uncle Mort's cupboard. She must've fed the stray cat. She rises and scoops up the can and slams the foul mackerel at the veranda wall, an improvisation, a desperate moment, free of deliberation, or so it seems. Later he'll overhear her telling Sophie, "I just wasn't on my best behavior."

What was the nature of his parents' marriage? Joe still wonders if there is a secret to marriage he hasn't discovered. His father's family was put off by the Bohemians his mother came from. "Too much goddamn hugging," his father said, of her family.

Did his parents hold hands companionably? Did they have sex when they were in their fifties and sixties? Or was it only now that people expected a lifetime of that? Did grief over his brother dying divert their love?

Once a year his father took his mother in the Skylark out to Lyons, to a nightclub, Mangam's Chateau. He knew someone out there who treated them well. "We ate *lobster*, Joey," his mother would say. "Dipped in garlic butter. I've come a long way from the girl who got off that ship in Baltimore in 1907 and worked in the glass factory." They danced to Jimmy Dorsey at Mangam's Chateau. His father would sing a Dorsey tune, not *to* his mother, but within earshot, when he was slapping on aftershave or adjusting his tie.

The glow of sunset in the summer skies,
The golden flicker of the fire flies,
The gleam of love light in your lovely eyes,
These are the things I love.

Mangam's Chateau burned to the ground in the seventies. They still had a chorus line then. A headliner. A comic. People dressed to the nines. Did the women smell like Tabu, a perfume his mother saved for special occasions?

The realtor gets out and tugs down her skirt. She isn't wearing sturdy shoes, either.

Arms akimbo, Emma says, "Joe. What's with you?"

Joe says, "This is not an isolated incident." Then something, the shadow that crosses her chin or the perplexed look in her eyes, makes him remember what she said last night.

Benny had gone; it was past midnight; Joe had fallen asleep in the recliner, a bowl of pretzels on his lap. A television commercial barked out the price of hot tubs. The news was on. Satchmo snoozed on the sofa.

Emma came in and took his hand and said, "Hi, sweetheart." She shrugged off her coat. "Is Benny here?"

Joe shook his head no. He had a hard time finding his voice; he was groggy.

She said, "He forgot his jacket."

He pressed the lever and the recliner jerked upright. He felt ashamed for her to find him dozing, with the TV on. It seemed so old-mannish. He said, "You look like someone new. In that sweater." She had borrowed a soft pink sweater from her friend Tiff, a younger woman. She had wanted to look younger when they decided at the last minute to go out to the blues bar after school. He knew all of this about her, without her saying so. And she did look younger: fit from swimming three times a week, glowing from her favorite drink: top-shelf margaritas. She examined every finger on his hand; she did not want to let go. His grip felt weak. "I'm glad to see you," he said. But he didn't know if that were true.

Emma said, "Where's my best friend? I want my best friend back."

She had hit him a fly and he screwed it up. Drifted so far away that he might as well have been a rookie daydreaming in the outfield. He thinks: long-term memory, short-term memory. He would have to work his way backward to make amends for the loss of that one short-term memory. If he decides to make amends. The entire day has been out of kilter because he did not recall her coming home the night before. The honest, raw catch in her voice when she said, "I miss my best friend. I want my best friend back."

He thinks of what Liz always says when she and Sophie have quarreled and she wants to make up. "Our ground time will be brief." Such trial and error wears on him.

The realtor picks her way to the veranda, her open-toed green shoes taking on brushstrokes of mud with each step, grinning like

a woman about to make some fast money. A green shamrock spar-
kles on her blazer. She tips her sunglasses to the top of her head
and declares, "It's the pot of gold. End of the rainbow, yes?"

EMMA COMPARTMENTALIZES IN IRELAND

MEMORIAL DAY, Emma and Joe March strolled around the cemetery, laying flowers here and there, trying to carry on a normal conversation, but finding it necessary to shout into the wind. They confirmed something they'd each privately mulled over: he would forego her dream trip to stay behind in Chicago with their grieving daughter Sophie.

Emma blurted, "You never wanted to go." A caravan of motorcycles va-roomed by, the riders decked out in bandanas and leather and chrome rivets. An odor from a shop—caustic solvent—rolled over the cement wall at one edge of the cemetery. If only the setting had been different. More subdued. She might have been able to convey her loss. Instead she sounded sulky.

His Cubs cap blew off and caught up on a wreath of plastic flowers. He stumbled to retrieve it, a little unsteady. Moles had tunneled in and around the graves; the ground was rutty. He ran his hand over his sugar-white hair and settled the cap firmly on his head. "No sense denying it," he shouted. It was the first time since Luis died that they had let fly their chronic disagreements. What selfish liberty. Emma thought: *No sense denying it* will be chiseled on your gravestone. Following on that, her heart hurt to see him stumble. There it was again: their age difference. "Give it a rest," she wanted to say when Joe found reason to mention it, even obliquely. Calling out Boomers for their conspicuous consumption or self-centeredness. "And me?" he'd say. "I'm old. Not even a War Baby. I'm a Depression Baby."

*   *   *

Now it's mid-June. Emma will spend a week in Ireland and then go on to Locarno, where she and Joe met decades ago. Traveling alone she might be transformed; she might return feeling whole. A three-times-a-week swimmer, Emma is a slim 7th grade teacher in her mid-fifties. She carries her diaphragm in her cosmetic bag for sentimental reasons.

The big-bellied plane is stuck in Dublin on the tarmac, waiting for a gate. There is the foul odor of the toilets to contend with. An Irish song—"The Town I Loved So Well"—crackles from the plane's loudspeakers. Emma pops a breath strip, a greenish paper-thin rectangle, into her mouth. The passenger next to her—an elderly Irish woman—reaches for her glasses in a hard shell case stowed in the mesh pocket. They talked a little, heading out of O'Hare. Emma did not tell the woman about her grief, even though the woman had been to a funeral in Joliet. They might have passed much of the night telling stories, comparing notes on grief and getting over grief. But where would Emma's begin and end? Not talking about it was freeing, an escape. She felt contrite, undeserving of such freedom.

The pilot in his radio-smooth brogue reassured them, yet during the flight Emma found herself gripping the armrest. If only she had been able to grab Joe's hand. She felt lonely in the turbulence. In spite of all they have been through, she had hoped for cuddling and possibly sex with Joe on the trip. And the sweetness after. It has been eight months since he reached for her near midnight. Her orgasms are not as seismic as they once were, but still, it's a tonic—she feels healthy and years younger afterwards. Her cheeks rosy. When was the last time he kissed her mouth?

A splash of tomato juice stains her khaki skirt. The last time she made her way to the restroom she looked gaunt, her complexion sallow. Never mind. The trip has begun with a mental leap ahead to a shower, or bath. To Danny's flat. Danny, her former student. His family had returned to Ireland at the end of 7th grade, and for twenty years, in annual holiday cards, Danny had insisted that Emma "come across the big pond" to visit his homeland. Under her tutelage Danny had grown confident about writing, and for that his parents were grateful. Will Danny's exuberance be contagious?

The bittersweet end-of-school events—dances and outings—were exuberant. It would have been a perfect June with her students if not for what she'd been through at home.

Since.

They rarely say *since Luis died.* Instead they say, Since that night. Since this. The word *this* a veil for the crush of daily waking up to it, crying in corners of the house, the failure of language to come to their aid. And for Emma, the corrosive worry about Sophie. Who blames her for not moving them out of the neighborhood where Luis was shot. A motiveless killing, the police and journalists surmise. Her worry about Sophie jerks Emma this way and that. You plan a trip for a year and then your beloved son-in-law dies a month before your departure. It sounds like one of those ethical puzzles in a magazine. Something you never imagine happening to you.

She wants Danny to rescue her.

She misses the banter of Luis and Sophie, the trickle of tango throughout the house. She has always considered herself intergenerational in her connections. A former colleague plans to move into an age 55-plus apartment complex in a few weeks and Emma does not get the point of that. Ordinary trees flat-line in the distance below the industrial haze of Dublin. She berates herself: for this I left my daughter?

The plane swings into its gate. The bell dings and with a collective sigh people are up and chattering and hauling luggage from the overhead bins. One steward says to another, "I could use a pint, but my Mum's waiting."

Emma doesn't have to cooperate or explain things to Joe, a relief. Juggling her purse and bag, finding the Blue Express Bus—everything works out the way she imagined it would. Once not long ago, Joe griped, "How did we manage when we were young? Why was it so important to us?" He meant: Why did we teach abroad?

Why did we make life complicated? And she said, "If you hadn't been teaching in Switzerland, we'd have never met."

Joe was supposed to say, "We'd have met somehow," or "That's the reason we went to Switzerland." Or some such affirmation.

But matter-of-factly Joe said, "No, we wouldn't have." As if that would have been no big deal. She holds this against him; she recalls that conversation at odd moments, brushing her teeth or serving cafeteria duty.

Dublin trundles by. Pubs with their bright red facades. Butcher shops and cricket fields. But she has little attention for it. She wanted Sophie to absolve her. To say, "It's all right. Don't give up your trip." Instead, she chewed Emma out. And Emma deserved it. No getting around that. She had violated their space, the third-floor bedroom and studio. If she had the house to herself Emma would slip out of her shoes and scoot in stocking-feet through the cat-disturbed hallway, its throw rugs furled up, toy balls scattered. Luis often left a lamp on and it cast a wedge of light on the steep stairway. Her face would burn with shame and apprehension. The photographs on the wall beside the stairs were staggered, a gallery of the girls in Easter dresses and formals and graduation gowns. That saturated surreal color, a grainy surface. Odd that these are the moments we save. In memory, other times are more indelible. Sophie at the Art Institute all those Saturdays, mute before Cezanne's basket of apples. And Liz, dear unhappy Liz, at baseball games with Joe; he would decode the umpire's calls; she watched him anxiously for clues. Liz was older and felt that Sophie got all the attention. Another impasse Emma failed to remedy.

All she ever did was stand before the easels. *Oak Street Beach. Good Friday/San Pio. Ashland Avenue/Winter. The Pizza Maker,* a 3 x 5 canvas of a man sliding a pizza into an oven, his arms muscular, the fire like the light of a brass foundry, something burnished, work with dignity, as Sophie sees it. The studio smells of linseed oil and paint, garlic and marijuana, shampoo and something else, bouquet of them.

She is not the kind of mother who snoops into their personal things, their CDs, their love notes, whatever they might have hidden in the bedside table drawers. All she wanted was to see

Sophie's work-in-progress. "That *is* personal," Sophie said, grimacing. Sophie's eyes that day were unforgiving. She said, "Why didn't you move us away from here?"

Emma gets off the bus, and it's chilly out, windy morning. At the curb, when the driver has hauled her bag from the luggage compartment, she tips him and begins the trudge two blocks east on Talbott, a street reminiscent of their Chicago neighborhood, with hole-in-the-wall music stores painted matte black inside and groceries with dingy windows. And yet, it does not seem like a district where people are shot on any evening. She passes Sophie's blame on to Joe, a permanent condition. Pilsen is where he grew up; their building—the shop and the flat above—had belonged to his grandparents, immigrants from the old country, scrambling for a toehold over one hundred years ago. She stops at a newsstand to buy cigarettes, a half-pack of Silk Cuts. She craves her one-a-day.

Pansies spill from a basket in the little patch-of-grass yard at Danny's. At the youth hostel next door a sandwich board on the sidewalk announces the Irish breakfast. Young people lounge about on the steps. Tattooed and pierced. The boys have scruffy beards; the girls' fingernails are painted blue or black. They could be the children of the men and women Emma traveled with around the Caribbean in her early twenties, right after she graduated from Oberlin. Or perhaps they are the grandchildren of those people— she hurriedly dismisses this notion without doing the math.

The young women bring to mind the affairs she had then. In the Caribbean, in Mexico. Pre-AIDS days. Before the teaching job in Locarno. How she and a boy would go on road trips or mail boat trips to visit friends and upon arriving they would throw down their sleeping bags and tell their friends, "We need to go to bed for a while," and they would close the door and fuck. No questions asked. No alibis. This is a memory she would have squelched if Joe had been beside her. Later they would rise and clean up and wander out to the living room in their shorts and T-shirts and there would be joints to smoke and reggae and rum. Marrying was the farthest thing from their minds. They sought a defiant sensorial field—what her mother would have skinned her alive for if she'd known.

Sometimes she thinks: It's a miracle I didn't catch something. Sometimes she thinks: Thank God I was a slut while I had the chance. But since her daughters came into the world, those years seem potentially dangerous. Like scaling a wall of memory with concertina wire looped along the top.

Emma rings the bell. Someone peeks out the window, cuffing back the lace curtain. A young, dark-haired woman opens up, wearing a beaded choker and a velvet blazer over a slinky rayon skirt. Her leather sandals are too rough, too sporty, for the outfit. Frosty blue smears her eyelids.

"Mrs. March, it is, isn't it?"

"Katie?"

"Aye, I'm Katie."

"Is Danny home?"

"Danny's not here, Mrs. March—"

"Call me Emma," Emma whispers. "You were expecting me, weren't you?"

"Aye, we were. We were."

Katie steps out onto the porch, which is more of a landing, crowded. A whistling man walks by with a St. Bernard on a leash. Katie leans toward Emma, confidentially. She doesn't like Katie; she's not sure why.

"I'm not gonna feed you a spoonful, Mrs. March. Danny's not the man you thought he was. He's run off. With another girl."

Ah, Katie, bearer of bad tidings. Emma says, and she wants to sound sincere, wants to *be* sincere, "Katie, I'm sorry."

"No one's sorrier than me. But he made arrangements. You're to go out to his mother's in Glendalough. He'll come visit you. He sees his mother quite a bit, he does. Every blade of grass and bit of gorse's precious to her. It's Wicklow. I can't take you in. You wouldn't expect that, now, would you, after he's left me."

Her brass earrings—parentheses—dangle around her cheeks. She's stalwart in the doorway of the flat, arms crossed. Beyond her sail rosettes of kitchen odors, caramelized onions and sausage.

"How far is…Glendalough?"

"Not so far. I'll help you find the bus. St. Kevin's bus. It goes twice daily from St. Stephen's Green. You'll get a taste of Grafton Street."

From within Katie's skirt pocket a cell phone rings melodically, bah-bah, black sheep. She turns her back to Emma and answers the phone. "I'll *be* there. Not to worry." Drama rolls off Katie like smoke from a burning house.

What would Joe say? He'd tug at her hand, pull her down the steps. "What're we doing, Emma? We could find a hotel. Decide for ourselves."

"We came here to see Danny, to see Danny's Ireland."

What is she to make of these phantom dialogues with Joe? Does he hear her speaking, too?

Katie grabs her suitcase. They set off, Katie chattering. "Dublin's *the big smoke* to the natives," she says. "You'll breathe easier out in the hills."

They circle around the Customs House and weave through a construction site. Block after city block, toward St. Stephen's Green, Katie catches Emma up: Danny writes for a travel magazine; he went to London to do a piece on theatres being restored; he met a woman—a TV personality—and when he came home, it was over. "She has a charmin' cottage in a *mews* near Hyde Park," Katie says. "She's the *mews-y* type, she is. With family money. When these things happen you have to find a reason."

"Yes, you do," Emma says. "But sometimes the reason's buried. There's so much sediment to dig down into."

Katie harrumphs. She hasn't a clue about sediment.

At the bus stop other passengers wait, surrounded by threadbare duffels and backpacks. Katie hands her a scrap of paper: Danny's mother's name—Rosaleen O'Neill—and a phone number. Emma remembers her in school-bus-yellow rain boots all those years ago; she thinks of his father in country-tweeds at a parent-teacher conference, his elbow on her desk, saying, "Danny's the best boy, don't you think?" Rosaleen had pursued a friendship with Emma and they met a few times for tea at a creperie on North Clark. Emma had felt constrained by the need to be professional, and at the end of the school year, when she might have opened up to her, the family returned to Dublin.

While they wait, Katie lights a cigarette and Emma wants one, too, but she has her rules. Katie says, "You're to call her. She'll fetch you."

She can't quite hide that she is sloughing Emma off.

Emma climbs aboard the St. Kevin's bus and Katie is gone, cutting into the crowd. In front of a department store, four girl violinists in jeans play a classical piece she catches a fragment of. Their violin cases laid out before them, the royal blue lining dotted with coins. She wishes she'd been able to drink in the music. Why did she allow herself to be bossed around? The trip has taken its toll on her brain—jet-lagged, sluggish.

Once she dozes.

Once she looks up Glendalough in her guidebook. There's a monastery ruin. A national park. Two lakes. Hiking trails.

She thinks of the floor plan of the National Gallery of Ireland; she downloaded it from the Internet at school and nearly memorized parts of it. She wanted to see Mary Swanzy's "Pattern of Rooftops." Since she was a young woman, the existence of orange-dull tile rooftops has cheered her, like the presence of palm trees or the scent of unfamiliar spices. She imagined sitting before Mary Swanzy's rooftops in the museum's subdued light. Hoping the absence of Joe would be tolerable in an art museum. Hoping she wouldn't miss Sophie too much. But the unexpected has begun, and so soon. Is it an omen of what's to come? Joe doesn't approve of omens and premonitions. Or the desire for dissimilarity as a means to wake up.

And what of Rosaleen, a widow now? What, if anything, do they have in common?

Before these thoughts gain unbearable traction, she is swept up in the arrival of the bus, with the ancient monastery in ruins to the north, the lakes brown as stout, the greenery profuse—scotch pine and gorse, little blue flowers and puffy white flowers (she yearns to discover their names)—and a wooden sidewalk zigzagging across the blanket bog and heath, leading toward the lakes. The sky is smaller here, and bubbling with clouds suddenly. A light drizzle begins. She expected that; the guidebook prepared her for rain nearly every afternoon.

Mary Swanzy, Irish painter, lived to be 96 years old. Did she come here? Was she free to contemplate the monastery? What would it be like to live forty-odd more years with her present anxieties hounding her? For she intends long life. Just not the life she has right now.

In the time it takes Emma to use the restroom, Rosaleen arrives in a blue panel van, a blue like a dusting of snow, with *Gram's Garden* faded on its side. She's wearing rubber boots and her knee patches are damp and her hands dry from digging down deep into soil. She grows flowers and tends gardens for lodges and restaurants. She seems familiar. But that word *Gram* alarms Emma. Rosaleen sees herself as a Gram. Emma never sees herself that way. She is not ready to be a grandmother. Joe, with his summer tomato plot, would have liked Rosaleen.

Reflexively, as women do, they seek out common ground in the first five minutes. Their love of the hills and mountains. Breakfast preferences. Covertly, Emma feels abrasive toward Rosaleen, the way she does sometimes with women her own age, guessing that Rosaleen is a lonely widow with no sense of adventure.

Her voice flannelly-rich with care, Rosaleen says, "You must be sleepy." She eases the van up the steep driveway. Down below, wooly sheep meander and bleat. Walkers in bright parkas crisscross the bottomland and the hills above the lakes.

Emma stifles a yawn. "I am—but I need to push through and sleep tonight."

"It's only three o'clock," Rosaleen says, checking her watch. "My dog's about to whelp. There's a bit of excitement to keep you up."

And so it is. Her dog—Molly, a Border collie with silver paws—lies in a padded dog bed behind a cylindrical Swedish stove. The stove is white and ornamented with flowers. Molly curls on her side and whimpers persistently—not quite a howl. Rosaleen kneels on a foam gardening pad and brings each slippery pup to Molly's face and Molly licks each one dry, even as she's giving birth to the next.

Outside the wind picks up. A true rain hammers the metal roof. "Dogs and houses," Rosaleen says, "are the passions of older women." Then, "Lashing, it is! Take down the Redbreast. Have a nip."

Emma had thought she would offer tea. "Maybe an inch." Fingerprints smudge the Redbreast bottle. Garden soil, Emma surmises. She pours them each a glass of whiskey. The burn feels cleansing and brings on the urge for a smoke. In a disinterested tone she says, "When do you think Danny'll come?" It would be unseemly to speculate about Danny, to be as playful in speaking about him as she might have been with him. They had exchanged playful emails. Being relegated to Glendalough was about acting her age.

Rosaleen laughs. "When he comes, he comes." She brushes her springy hair from her forehead, tucks it behind one ear. Her complexion is ruddy, with a web of thread-like red lines on one cheek. She makes no effort to change the shape of her bushy eyebrows. "I hope you'll be content. Danny said you'd be wanting to walk."

Danny won't come to Glendalough: Emma knows that now. They might have returned to Dublin. She had hopes pinned on Danny that she hadn't been entirely aware of. Something vague about him and his girlfriend taking her out to a club, treating her like a youngish aunt. More escape. "Who wouldn't be content here?" she says. "Thank you for having me."

"You know—I don't like you're missing Dublin. Day after tomorrow I've a training there. If you like, we'll go together. I'll drop you in the city."

A possible crossroad, but Emma can't say what she wants. The pups wriggle against Molly's teats. With both hands, Rosaleen gently rolls and settles them. Nursing, they sound tiny, squeaky. "You'd be free to change your plans. Or come back here." Rosaleen sits back on her heels and sips her whiskey, assessing Emma. "If you take a liking to it."

"What sort of training?"

Rosaleen nods to a photo on the wall: she's in a red mountain parka, snowy hills beyond. "Helicopter training," she says. "I'm on the Rescue Team."

Certain items in the kitchen come into focus: a rucksack, a helmet, flares.

"The Coast Guard's drilling us." Her eyes light up. "In a Sikorsky S61. We learn to embark, disembark. We learn to unload stretchers with the winch."

"That's…daring."

"I like the lads who do it. We work together." Rosaleen plucks up another newborn with a pink snout. "That makes five. Molly, Molly," she croons. "What a good girl."

Then: "Tomorrow night my goddess group meets in Coolboy. At the Little Moon pub. Maybe you'd like to go with."

"What's goddess group?"

"Hestia's big in me. The hearthkeeper. Or Brighid to us Irish. But she's nagged by Artemis. A bully who only wants to be on Rescue Team." Rosaleen laughs. "I went to school with some of the girls. We're not strict about where the goddesses come from. We mix and match. We talk about who rules us. Or who creates our torments—what troubles us."

She might become someone new. Among women. Talking about women. "I'd like that," Emma says. Brief buoyancy comes over her. She thinks that it will all work out. By *it* she means her struggle to re-enter her marriage. To feel at one with Joe again.

"I thought you might."

Emma eyes the black telephone wired to the wall. She calculates time zones. It's nearly five in Ireland—before lunch in Chicago. "I need to call home," she says. "I have a phone card."

"Feel free. Anytime," Rosaleen says. She smiles over her shoulder, puppy legs dangling from one hand. "You remind me of who I was then."

"We're not those women anymore," Emma says. The rain intensifies, makes her claustrophobic. She pours another inch of Redbreast.

"Well, sure, we're better."

"I was thirty-five then," Emma says. "I loved life."

Cross-legged beside Molly, Rosaleen waits for the afterbirth. "And now?"

From the kitchen table, Emma tells her about Luis. "We should have left the neighborhood. We should've. When the girls were born."

"I'm so sorry," Rosaleen says. "Why didn't you?"

"Joe's stubborn. I hate the commute. Hate it." Emma slips out of her flats. Two toes are blistery red. Vanity, vanity. She should have worn the round-toed walking shoes in her suitcase. Should,

should. Now she'll pay the price. "I've wanted to move for a long time." She pictures Joe at his uncle's farm, the hope she saw on his face. A kind of erasure of what ails him. She thinks: Not there. I don't want to move to the country. I never will. Liz calls the city the behavioral sink, referring to an experiment with female rats; the mama rats raised their young in the corners of a maze but went down into the open area in the center of the maze—the behavioral sink—to misbehave.

Rosaleen muses tentatively, "Danny always says hate's a very strong word."

Emma smiles. "Danny would." She does not take it as a reprimand.

Rosaleen says, "I've learned a few things from Danny, I have."

"Aren't you ever lonely?" Emma says.

The fluids of birth darken Rosaleen's trousers. Her face is flushed. "I never am," she says.

All night Emma thrashes. During dinner she drank a little more whiskey. Now the aftermath, a rough-around-the-edges feeling compounded by jet lag. She is not alone; it's a fallacy to think that a mother can travel alone. If you have children, you're never quite whole again. There's a reason why they're called your flesh-and-blood—gobbets and shavings, crumbs and scraps of your body careen across life's stage like Tinkerbell on rollerblades. What mother doesn't wait for phone calls?

She telephoned home right before bed. No one answered, and she left a message explaining her whereabouts and leaving the new number. Adding softly, "Love to hear your voice, Sophie." She wonders how she sounds to them. Light-hearted? Resentful? Tired of the curtain of greenish, dense rain? And what does she mean by *them?* Who will listen to the message?

At breakfast she says to Rosaleen, "I meant for a man. Aren't you ever lonely for a man?"

The light in the kitchen is watery, cool. Out the French doors, rainwater accumulates in clay pots where the soil has absorbed all it can. Rosaleen sets a basket of buttered toast on the table. She wears a warm bathrobe.

"I thought I might be," she says. "After Bertie died."

Emma decided against packing a bulky bathrobe. She's dressed for the day already in jeans and a sweater, but she envisions going back to bed with a mystery from the shelf of paperbacks in her room. Her toes are definitely blistered, painful.

She says, "When was that?"

"Five years ago this past Christmas."

"I'm sorry."

Rosaleen nods to acknowledge Emma's sympathy. "After two years I woke up and thought that company might be a good thing. Not a soul mate. A movie date."

Emma laughs.

"I had a few. Movie dates, that is."

"And?"

"I took them as interruptions. No fault of their own, really. I didn't want to have to get dolled up and think about what *they* wanted and whether *they* were happy with me. Those're habits of mind hard to change. Trying to please. All that."

All that.

She likes Rosaleen and then she doesn't. A see-saw. A terrible way to experience hospitality. Around noon, the rain tapers off and the sun comes out. Rosaleen offers her bandages for her toes and rubber garden clogs so that she may help in the garden. Planting coriander seeds and basil and carrots. When Emma pushes the wheelbarrow of compost, hurry-scurry, Rosaleen says, "No need to be lively. It's not a job that's ever finished." She didn't realize she'd been hurrying. She worried: What am I hurrying toward and why? Her mind leaps ahead to Locarno, where Zubin—old friend, headmaster—awaits her visit.

After lunch she attempts to telephone home; again, no one answers. Sophie doesn't answer her cell phone and Joe refuses to carry a cell phone. Where are they, at seven in the morning? She dawdles over coffee, nibbles an apple turnover, listens to the news on the radio. Sunlight crosshatches the wood floor.

After a mirthful commotion at the front door, a man nearly leaps into the kitchen with Rosaleen right behind. Bearded, with curling gray hair, wearing broken-in boots and a chambray shirt. He's around Emma's age. Meaning, somewhere between forty-five and fifty-five. She can't tell. He has a wen—a small scarlet tumor like a bird's egg—on one cheek. Rosaleen says, "My brother, Liam. From Galway. Emma March. Emma's visiting from Chicago."

Liam invites her on a ramble above the lakes. "Unless it sounds too much like a forced march," he says, winking at Rosaleen.

"Make no mistake," Rosaleen says, "it'll be a forced march."

"Sounds lovely," Emma says.

"She's got blisters," Rosaleen says. "Don't be hard on her."

They go, with Emma's toes on fire. Rainwater evaporates in smoky tendrils upward from the ground. Other walkers emerge from cottages and the big hotel. There is the sense of all things new after the rain, a frolic.

And there's something perfect about Liam. The perfection of someone you don't know but you might get to know.

He is a glass-blower, divorced, with an ex-wife he still sees once a month. An amiable arrangement. "We had our grudges. But they seem to have disappeared. We get on fine." He comes to Glendalough to sell his glass to the shop in the hotel.

Emma pries: "If you get on so well, why…?"

"We never really spoke the same language." He turns and grins. They are proceeding up a long grade, on a gravel road. He takes the opportunity to catch his breath, a hand on his chest, the other waving away invisibilities: His ex? His memories? His doubts? "Oh, she *speaks* English. But, well, she wears a hardhat at work. She works in a Mini assembly plant."

"A hardhat."

"That seems to exemplify our differences." He marches on beside her. He takes her hand, but not in a flirty way, merely friendly; she pulls it back.

He asks about her family. "Two grown girls. And my husband has a shop beneath our flat. He sells baseball memorabilia.

To collectors." She will not tell him about Luis. She pretends to breeziness, joie de vivre.

"Expensive stuff?"

"Indeed," Emma says.

They ramble for nearly two hours until he does something she finds disconcerting. He has taken out a lumpy, well-used handkerchief from his back pocket. He's a nose-blower, very loud. "Allergies," he apologizes. She wants to ask him if he has a new significant other, to take the focus off the mucous-y handkerchief. He seems to read her mind and volunteers, "I date three different women." He offers thumbnail sketches of each: a barmaid with a degree in engineering; a painter with three children; a widow ten years older.

"And do they date three different men, as well?" It sounds like a telephone tree in an emergency.

"At our age, we're not that interested in settling down. Why should we?"

Emma is put in the awkward position of defending settling down, when she herself has asked that very question, recently, lying abed next to Joe.

"For companionship?" she offers.

"Yes, yes," he says absent-mindedly, for he has stopped to admire a crop of flowers growing out of stone, tough, lavender, shaped like stars. He charms her again with his boyish enjoyment. Joe was once like that. Then and now—her thoughts of Joe bifurcate into then and now.

By the time they are coming down the switchbacks, into the twilight, he has invited her to dinner at the hotel, where, he promises, there will be a piano player. A local farmer. Liam describes the old man, his misshapen hands, his red suspenders. As if every detail is cause for celebration. She feels the pinch of having already made plans. A little white lie might be necessary. "Let me see how I'm feeling."

On the footbridge over the frisky creek, right before they reach the narrow blacktop, Liam says, "This's been grand."

The exertion of the walk has given her wings. Her calves are shapely; her joints loose as if well-oiled. "It has," she says.

Back at the house, a note is tacked to her door: *Your husband telephoned. He'll try to call back later.* What exactly does "try" mean? In the intimate, too-tight hall, with its tallboy dresser and framed prints of sheepdogs and oak trees, Liam has to squeeze past her to get to his room. He aims to touch her lower back, a gentlemanly gesture, but in the close quarters, his hand grazes her hip. To her, an electric sensation. He is a man accustomed to having his women within reach. He says, "So you're free for dinner?"

Folding the foolscap note in half, Emma says, "My daughter's calling later." Big sigh of resolve, a false smile. "I've been wanting to talk with her. I think I'll have a bite here, after all."

"Another time, then."

Emma glances into his bedroom, lit by a rouge sunset. A tartan flannel shirt shrugs off the rocking chair. There's a stack of folded clean handkerchiefs on the dresser.

"Wait right there, right there," he says. Liam turns into his room, bends low into a crate. He comes back with a pebbly glass plate the size of a bar of bath soap: red and purple, with gold triangles in each corner. A jewel. "Take this home with you. To remember our walk."

"You're very kind."

"Likewise."

She seeks out Rosaleen in the damp garden. "I'd better not go to Coolboy."

Rosaleen leans on a pitchfork handle. She is utterly of the land, as if she sprouted there among the raspberry canes. "Naturally, you want to hear their voices. It's a hard time, sure, and you're a long way from home."

Later, Emma lies on the bed, smoking and reading. The smoke, most of it, glides out the open window. Her blisters pulse. She strains to interpret the jocular give-and-take of Rosaleen and Liam. Then the rush of water in the pipes as they take turns bathing. Someone turns on music she recognizes: big band, Ray Anthony, wartime, her parents' music. Finally, Rosaleen knocks on her door and says, "I'm off to goddess group. Root around in the icebox for dinner."

After her bath, and changing into a flowered skirt and white blouse, Emma ferrets out a leftover slice of mushroom pie. Half-heartedly, she reads a gardening magazine Rosaleen has left lying about; her dinner under tinfoil heats in the toaster oven. The puppies suckle in the dog bed. Liam pops his head into the kitchen and says, "I'll be leaving early in the morning. If I don't see you, safe journey." Unrelentingly cheerful are words she would put to him, if she ever had reason to tell anyone.

"Oh. Yes, thank you. I enjoyed the day." She thinks, "Take me with you. Take me to your leader. *Abduct me.*"

She eats her homely mushroom pie in the near dark. The telephone rings just as she has washed her plate and set it in the dish rack.

Joe says, "Emma. How's it going?" She has antennae for his moods; this call is perfunctory. She remembers what a therapist on TV once said: "The ability to withstand disappointment portends a long marriage." Is that ability like your immune system, degraded with age?

"How's Sophie?"

Joe waits a beat, then: "We don't run into each other much."

"I feel like she's hiding. Or hiding something."

"Emma."

"What?"

"You worked hard to get where you are. You want to have a good time, right?"

"Of course."

"Compartmentalize, then."

Advice from Joe. That's novel.

When they hang up, Emma goes out to the kitchen balcony and smokes another cigarette. What she remembers is falling in love.

Zermatt, years ago, arriving there in June, before the season began, to wait for Joe. She had finished her first year teaching at the Swiss boarding school near the Italian border. Joe had taught art there for years. He had made a prior arrangement to visit a friend passing through Geneva, but Emma had gone on to Zermatt. She watched the fair Swiss women kneel and plant their annuals along the stone walkways. 1973. She wanted Joe so badly she could think of little else; at night she had tossed and turned half-asleep for months; the memory of his smell—the waxy crayons, the charcoal sticks, and beneath that, a slightly ripe grainy odor; he was a health nut then, not an aficionado of donuts as he is now—that memory would beset her as soon as she lay down to sleep in her room on the third floor of the girls' dormitory, where she had been stationed to be a good role model. Virtuous, studious, thrifty, and kind. She willed him to wash the porcelain slip from his hands and come to her window. He would ping the glass with gravel and she would open the window and they would speak in stage whispers and in code. The students might be eavesdropping. Later, the liquid moon seeped in; what hormones rushed along inside her, spree of desire.

Some memories disperse like steam; some she will never forget. People warned her about getting involved with a man so much older, but she did not take heed.

How easy it is, she thinks, to be judgmental. Other people's lapses, their sea changes, appear daft or unfair. Danny running off to London, for instance.

Like love, drifting away from Joe seems to come at her from outside her ken, a force visited upon her—by what goddess?

The telephone rings once more and she answers. This time it's Sophie, telling her tales of Satchmo, their old cat. She feels the grip of betrayal; Sophie is being a good daughter, but Emma has foregone being a mother. For now. Just now. Sophie says, "Ems. Enjoy yourself. You deserve it." And in one chamber of her heart, a weight lifts; absolution has been set before her, if only she can bear to take it.

She goes up to her room and turns on the desk lamp and takes out a pristine journal. What married woman of a certain age hasn't thought about what she would do if she were alone? If her postponed dreams were to emerge from the fog of wifely, teacherly, motherly routine? If post-menopausal zest could be worn like an estrogen patch? She writes the date in the journal. But after that, nothing comes except a doodle. Will it be necessary to justify her next move to Rosaleen?

She straightens her hair and adds a lick of lipstick. Then a cotton sweater. Outside, the night is neutral, not cool or warm. She is of the night. Gravel scratches beneath her feet. The wind picks up and moonlight riffles on the lake. The lights of the big hotel shimmer. Drawing nearer, she hears the piano, a lighthearted American tune: "Cheek to Cheek." She's wearing the flats, and they are tight. The bandage wrinkles up and she stops, leans against a tree, peels off the bandage, and tosses it into the woods. A slovenly gesture.

It comes to her—not all at once like a pearl of wisdom, but in distasteful increments—that complaints she has about Joe are little stories she tells herself to shore up her own desires. And walking down to find Liam, she blinks back tears, thinking—but not for long—of how she has deceived herself. And will.

EPHEMERA

AFTER HE DIED, for what seemed like a long time—more than a month—Sophie March-Gonzales could not speak his name. It felt frozen between her collarbones.

Her parents tried to get her to say his name without admitting to their task. They had ideas about grief. They were Catholic, but not so serious, even though Sophie's Great-Uncle Leo was a Dominican monk and had been arrested three times for civil disobedience in anti-war protests.

He had admired Uncle Leo, and Uncle Leo had suggested what he could do to make a difference—a homeboy come back to Chicago after going to college on a full-ride in a backwater town in South Dakota. He was only a few years older than the kids in gangs. Whenever gang-related episodes shook the neighborhood, he dashed to the emergency room and talked down the survivors. Talked them down from revenge. The people who did this work liked to say, "We have to get there before the blood dries on the pavement."

About Uncle Leo, her father said: Too much Vatican II in his veins. He and a Jesuit friend had sneaked onto an air base and taken a sledgehammer to a fighter jet. Sophie didn't care one way or the other—she wasn't that political and she wasn't that religious. She had been old enough to vote in 2004, but she didn't.

Where did her parents get their ideas? Possibly radio talk shows. They considered themselves progressive politically, but they did not believe you should break the law for a higher cause, as Uncle Leo did. She did not think about her parents much beyond everyday kindness, although, since the wedding not quite a year ago, they had lived with her parents, above her father's shop. She did not think about them, but they thought about her. She was their project, the younger of two daughters. Liz had split and they rarely heard from her.

He wasn't killed in the war; he had been murdered a block away, in front of the bike shop, the night of her mother's birthday and Cinco de Mayo. She had baked her mother a cake from scratch.

Her habitat had withered: the living room, the kitchen. She did not venture up to the third floor where his dress shirts hung like pastel files in the armoire, where her paints gave off a faint oily odor. She did not return to her work: the 3 x 5 canvas called *The Pizza Maker*. In the living room were two windows: out one, she saw St. Adelbart's bell tower in the distance, and nearby, staked on a roof, a hand-lettered plywood sign that read **the road to war was paved with lies**; out the other, a tamale café and a tuxedo rental shop with frothy First Communion dresses displayed on headless mannequins. And then down below, the flowers: glads and carnations, tulips and daisies. Some from florists, in green tissue, and some from garden strips along the alley, their stems wrapped in waxed paper and rubber bands. It had stormed—a big violent summer storm that she had watched evolving over the lake—and the flowers were a soggy vegetative mess. She went back and forth between the two windows, wringing her hands. She understood what it meant to feel like you were losing your mind.

At St. Adelbart's they still said Mass in Polish, but Sophie did not know a single Polish person in the neighborhood. That was another century. Her father called himself the last bohunk in Pilsen, but he was not one-hundred percent Bohemian. Their last name was March and her Grandfather March had come to Chicago from Liverpool and worked for Schwinn in Schwinn's heyday. Then he had started the baseball memorabilia business in a poor location, far from Wrigley Field, not close enough to Comisky.

The decisions of her family seemed capricious. *He* had wanted to make a good decision about where to live and she had disagreed with him, not sure about moving. They had been living with Sophie's parents to pay off school loans and live the bohemian life—small b.

When she stared at the bell tower, she thought of tango lessons in the church basement. Of him holding her and whispering, teasing: "Mother Teresa's got her eye on you, Soph." In church basements where they taught tango lessons, there would always be those icons, Mother Teresa, the Blessed Virgin. And Sophie aswirl in her dancing dresses and dancing shoes.

When they were twelve years old, servers at Mass, there had been covert, shy kisses in the sacristy at San Pio.

And a snowy afternoon when he took her to his mother's kitchen and fed her champurrado, deluxe hot chocolate that tasted like oranges and cinnamon.

On her birthday in April he had stuck a postcard in the corner of the bathroom mirror: a black-and-white photo of a broken-down building with a corrugated roof; the sign on the building read **CARNAL GARAGE**. From Carnal, Kentucky. He liked to say, "Carnal knowledge of you—that's part of my husbandly job description."

He loved it when she walked around the bedroom naked. Still, she had been bashful. She wasn't sure of herself physically and it had taken her months into marriage to feel secure walking around the bedroom naked. She wasn't like some girls. She wasn't like Liz.

In his arms, dancing in slo-mo to the tart Spanish guitar, what exhibitionist there was in Sophie flowered at tango. He called out the steps to their students who watched from a tentative circle. The checkerboard tile floor was a little gritty, not smooth as it should be. Buzzing florescent lights imbued their faces with a sickly tinge. A sexual current saturated her back with the pressure of his hand, his response to her ocho, her fluidity, the sharp ping of her heels on the floor. His cologne and the chemical reaction of it with his skin seduced her: the citric-tang of him.

These were private stories; no one would ever know. They had spent ten years—since they were twelve!—constructing a private world that she had assumed would reel on so far into the future that she did not have to consider its ending. She hunched at the window above the flowers, balling up tissues, tearing them apart. Impressions of him (she couldn't call them memories, that sounded more organized than she felt) were like a hot bath she had hoped would soothe her to the bone; instead, they scalded. Then she screamed. Then she flung herself down on the sofa and moaned.

*   *   *

A recycler, her mother had gathered up all the socks that needed darning. She piled them in a basket—over a dozen pair. Sophie and she had a tendency to wear out the toes; her father wore out the heels. The socks kept her mother's hands busy; she didn't want to nibble. She had become a woman who grazed, on peanuts, on dried papaya bits from the health foods store. Her mother was her witness, whether Sophie wanted a witness or not.

The kitchen counters and refrigerator shelves were laden with food brought by neighbors. By the bicycle repairman. By the cook at the Dominican priory. Enchiladas and casseroles. Peanut butter cookies. Food that made her skin crawl to look at it. Sophie did not eat for three days after the funeral; finally she craved chocolate. Her father went out for chocolate ice cream, chocolate bars. He laid in a supply of Benadryl; she would not leave home to go to the doctor to ask for a prescription to help her sleep.

When her mother couldn't find her darning egg, she substituted an egg-shaped paperweight of hand blown glass, given to Sophie on her wedding day, replica of an egg used by brides in the 19th century to cool their hands and keep them calm. An item she wanted to donate to the Goodwill, but her mother said she would regret it.

Sophie stood at the window in a T-shirt and stretchy work-out pants, pilly with bits of white cotton. Her complexion blotchy, eyes puffy. Her lips cracked. Her hair gathered into a mop with a tortoise shell clip. Down below, homemade crosses had appeared, messages on poster board, novena candles: a shrine lit by sunlight. The storm had blown east; the temperature was in the low seventies. A half-block away, a woman let go with a melodious curse in Spanish. The Blue Line rattled the windows in their frames. Once it passed, Sophie turned to her mother and said, "When I was a little girl, I wondered why we lived here." She spoke as if every word was a brick she had to carry to build a sentence.

Her mother said, "Did you?"

"Why did you agree to it?"

"Your father…he wanted it. It's his home. And…"

"What?"

"It made our lives affordable. Once he quit teaching." Her mother had always presented the prescribed united front, cleaving to the discipline of not blaming their father for anything. She said, "It felt temporary, sweetheart. I didn't think about the future."

"Now we're there, aren't we? This is the future you didn't think about." Sophie unfurled a sky blue yoga mat and sat down upon it. Her legs in a V, she leaned into a stretch, her chin nearly resting on one kneecap. She didn't want to be bitchy, but she felt colonized by an alien force.

"I thought it might make him happy," her mother said. "I wasn't very good at choosing what to go along with and what to fight."

"Why not, Ems?"

Sophie recalled a tipsy confession when her mother had come home from a night out with women friends. "I wanted my marriage above all else. I wouldn't cross your father when we were young. When *I* was young. Lately I feel like a widow." She had giggled to take away the self-consciousness of giving Sophie too much information.

Now, her mother said, "Do you really want to hear about that?"

Her father was much older than her mother. There was something amiss between her parents, some distance Sophie surmised. But that was their business. She said, "It's been the best and worst for me." The black cat Satchmo sniffed the edges of the yoga mat; he rubbed up against Sophie's thigh, his purr like a motor. Sophie shoved him away, spitting, "Piss off."

Patiently, her mother laid down her mending. The glass egg in an angora sock, the needle glinting at the toe. She went into the kitchen and opened a can of cat food and fed the cat.

When she returned, Sophie offered her a section of chocolate bar, the tinfoil peeled back. "I think you weren't ready to be a grandmother. Am I right?"

Her mother inhaled sharply. "Sophie."

She felt a mean satisfaction in hurting her mother. She wanted to lash out, to ignore the need for integrity. Lashing out trumped sorrow for a brief moment. "Am I right?"

Her mother blinked back tears. "I didn't think of it that way at all."

"Think of it now. Now that it's only theoretical." She had tried to talk them out of getting pregnant. She had tried to say they were too young. Her mother opened her arms; Sophie shook her head no. She said, "Don't go up to our room. That's our room."

Her mother knelt beside the sofa and gathered Sophie in. "I'm sorry."

But Sophie was stiff in her arms. "Why did you?"

"I wanted to see your work. That's all."

"Don't go up there anymore. That's private. You always said we have to respect each other's privacy. But you didn't." She said once more, because she could get away with it, "We're in the future you didn't want to think about."

This was Pilsen, how Sophie saw it: port of entry, lucky Chicago neighborhood not gutted by the great fire of 1871. Shoeshine men at Jumping Bean Café guzzled red-eye espressos, elbow to elbow at the counter with college gringas. She had been that college gringa, high on being herself, self-congratulatory, an art student in torn jeans, portfolio of sketches under her arm. Pilsen, where the streets once ran like a river of black cinders from the factories. A neighborhood with no Starbucks, Pilsen was the steamy odor of tortillas fresh from the conveyor, supermercados fragrant with mangos.

At Saint Pius V, San Pio, long ago an Irish parish, Father Roberto on Sunday morning shouted, "Viva Mexico! Viva la cultura de latinos y chicanos—" Where the new young mothers and fathers lined up after Mass with forty-day-old infants, and to the tumult of marimba and guitar, the pastor tucked the bottom of each infant in his palm and supported the delicate neck and hoisted each infant in the air and swept up to the altar, offering the infant to God. His Lady of Guadalupe vestments shining, white like the Easter lilies, he pivoted in a ceremonial circle to show the infant to the parish. The applause was like water. You swam in the applause for the babies.

Her Bohemian ancestors fled Eastern Europe and settled in Pilsen; they named Pilsen and joined together in sokols—gymnastic and social clubs—to nurture body and mind and spirit. If you were sick and could not work, a nickel would be collected from every sokol member to tide you over.

Sokols, Sunday Mass in Polish at St. Adelbart's, a religious arts store replete with every manner of Guadalupes for the devoted guadalupanas—plastic mini-shrines, T-shirts, pinkie rings—stocked alongside holy cards of Our Lady of Czestochowa, purported to be the oldest image of the Mother of God, painted by St. Luke and brought to Poland as dowry between two royal families: all Pilsen. And a stubble-faced drunk hobbling down the alley, crying, "Give me chiles, give me chiles." Pope John Paul II came to visit these streets, to bless the people. Vicente Fox came to ask for votes. In a black rodeo hat, on horseback, he flashed the V for victory sign. "Wheels, wheels, feet, feet, all day," Carl Sandburg wrote of Blue Island Intersection, not far from where Sophie's husband was murdered.

When she wasn't freaking out, she wondered when his name would thaw and she wondered where she would move, when she moved away.

Sophie had sighed into the early May afternoon, her mother's birthday. To test for doneness, she slipped a toothpick in the mound of each chocolate layer. Two hundred dollars in tips she had earned the night before—waiting tables—lay crumpled in a pasta bowl. Now her tired bones wanted to melt; she felt like the Silly-Putty he fiddled with when he tried to quit smoking.

What might she wear to the party—what was she going for? Demure, good daughter, baker of birthday cakes? Seductive wife? In spite of the raw weather Sophie had managed to tan by spending twenty minutes in a string bikini out in the courtyard on any recent sunny day. Sun fell at noon on the picnic table and she lay there on a yoga mat, determined to brown up.

Her mother's potholder mitts were thick and frayed; she

stuck her hands into them and slid the round cakes from the oven; the oven heat took the chill off her bare arms. Her mother had always dreamed aloud of summer birthday parties. Other years, hail bounced on cars like polka-dots. Sleet poured forth, gray as concrete. Today wasn't so bad. The men were down below in the courtyard, dressed in insulated work shirts, installing electric braziers in the trees to keep everyone warm. Her mother had walked to the health center for a swim.

Ambrosia of chocolate cake filled the kitchen. "We'll christen that courtyard when your folks go away," he said, coming in the kitchen door. Everyone said that lust disappears, but that had not been the case with them.

Blue pastel smeared across his forehead, remnant of the art class he taught at the museum. Sophie grinned. "You read my mind." Her parents were planning a trip to the Swiss town where they had been teaching when they met. A long-anticipated, long-saved-for dream trip.

He dipped into the fridge and took out a Corona. He offered it to her, but she shook her head no, with a shiver. Later she would think, Why? I wish I'd drunk from his bottle. It was crazy to regret that, but she did. Regret came in all sizes.

And then he said: "So what're you wearing?"

"You'll see. A surprise."

"Sophie loves surprises."

"You've got this—" Sophie waggled a finger in front of her own forehead to indicate the blue smear.

"Hey, sleepy-head," he proposed, "want to lie down for a few minutes?" And she played that over and over: hey, sleepy-head, hey, sleepy-head, hey, sleepy-head. Would she forget the sound of his voice? She felt it eroding like beach into the lake. She had little to replenish the sound of his voice: two messages she had saved on her cell.

He had stripped off his insulated shirt and draped it over the back of a chair. A Saint Chris medal gleamed against his white undershirt. He could tell you that Saint Christopher protects travelers and bachelors, boatmen, bookbinders, bus drivers, cab drivers, epileptics, fruit dealers, gardeners, porters, sailors, and anyone at all against lightning, hailstorms, toothache, and sudden death.

They went upstairs to their hideaway and closed the door and lay down fully clothed. Heat from the oven had risen from downstairs and still they nested together. This was one of the unexpected pleasures of marriage—the cocoon of napping together. Right before she fell asleep, her thoughts came down to one: if lust disappears, this will be a fine consolation prize.

St. Patrick's Day, a Saturday morning. He wants to make what he calls married love. Nookie is more about him, a quickie, hooking up in the bathroom with the shower running full bore to buffer any squeals. Married love is more about Sophie, with tango or Coleman Hawkins playing, Sophie in purple silk or some other slippery trifle. She has a closet full of chemises and slips and nightgowns, cottony, rayon, eyelet-trimmed, paisley, lace, be-ribboned and flounced. She likes to make love with her clothes streaming away, half-unbuttoned, a vixen in a Vargas illustration. Sophie is petite, with small breasts, hair she perms in a tangled wad down her back, and a heart-shaped face. The acknowledged beauty in the family.

In a summery nightgown. With the sheet pulled up over her breasts. She spoons syrupy mandarin oranges from a blue Japanese bowl first into his mouth, then her own. Church bells ring out. She sold two paintings yesterday. A quarter-bottle of flat champagne on the dresser testifies to their celebration.

His angularity presses against her softness. Like John Lennon and Yoko. Iconic lovers. His hard-on has a nickname: Señor Amor.

He says, "I think your mother was in here again."

"The White Shoulders gives her away."

He says, "Your Dad heard a shot in the alley last night."

Sophie can see where that might lead. Why doesn't she want to move? Liz thinks it's a cop-out, living with their parents.

She sets the empty bowl on the floor and gets up and goes to the window, saying, "I'll be—right back, dear-dude." Overcast light strikes her as faintly carotene or copper. Downstairs, her father calls out to her mother: "I'll pull the car around." At last. But her mother still putters. Sophie hears her talking to Satchmo, swatting a closet door shut. She imagines the neighborhood as if she were a putty-colored gull gliding off-course from Lake Michigan and able to survey the whole panorama, the Mexicano murals and the panaderias and the treeless streets.

He wants to move. Everyone leaves the neighborhood sooner or later, he tells her. That's the immigrant story.

It's the one big thing they disagree about.

Sophie's people were among the immigrants nearly one hundred years ago, and now her family inhabits the house like a ship about to go down. Her hardwood floors slant and she doesn't know exactly what that means, but it can't be good news.

He lies there in watch-plaid boxers. Her nightgown feels like a sunny day on a beach, like a coconut palm outside a sunny stucco room, outside a window trimmed in blue or yellow. They've been to places like that, spring breaks, Punta Cana and Cabo San Lucas. She unravels images. It is a fantasy nightgown. What you need at the tail end of a Chicago winter to keep from noticing your dry heels and the way static crackles in your hair. A cloudy day, the forecast calls for drizzle.

She lets the Venetian blind down with a clack. "We can't do anything about it. Not now." Then, "Señor Amor."

He reaches down and slips a CD into the player beside the bed. Some tango. "'Creole Courtyard,'" he says, grinning wickedly. "Soph. Want to make a baby? Listen to this. 'And in the tatters of some pretty half-moon, her dark face would gaze at me…'"

She lies across the bed and he pampers her. Eventually, astride him, Sophie works up a good sweat.

Liquor bottles shined and winked on the card table Sophie had dressed up with a sheet of rice paper flecked with bits of flowers. He pounded down the steps from the third floor, his hair damp, shirtsleeves rolled above his wrists, but he turned so precisely at the landing that he did not notice Sophie and her mother talking on the landing in the dusk. At the bottom of the stairs, he tucked a CD into the player and the courtyard was silken with "Unforgettable"—Natalie Cole.

Her mother murmured about the people she saw down below at her fifty-fifth birthday shebang. Shebang was what her father called it and Sophie liked the sound of that: mélange of music and scents and glasses tinkling with ice, laughter. Benny—old friend of her father's, a sweet, depressed sculptor in his fifties, one silver earring bright above his black turtleneck. Teachers and their dates from her mother's school. Uncle Leo. All good Democrats. She could predict that they would talk baseball and politics. At the rental hall across the alley, a gaggle of women gathered on the back porch. Their gossip in Spanish rose like a cloud and drifted.

Her father was a good dancer. At weddings women admired him, his sure-footed, light steps and the way he and her mother fit. It was one thing they always did well, no matter what else was going on. They all danced—even Liz and her odd, unknowable boyfriend, a Geek Squad agent with a faceful of chrome piercings. And for a moment, a song's worth, Sophie had the sense that they were bound together not by the March family roles but by what her mother—anticipating her trip—called *delizia*, a lust or zest.

Two weeks after the funeral, she dragged herself up and walked to his parents' house. She had been invited. Their house was empty of an afternoon. His mother taught a literacy class every day. His father was at the tire store. There was a note from his mother on the table: Sophie, dear. Help yourself to treats. Come see us on Sunday. We miss you. Come to Mass and dinner after.

She could imagine it. His mother crying at the sink, skeins of tears on her bronze cheeks. "When I'm with you, I can't help crying," she would say. "It's good for me." His grown sisters upstairs in their girlhood bedroom, with ballads from a radio station in Puerto Vallarta streaming from the computer. How could she sit there on the carpet in their bedroom, her skirt bunched up on her thighs, her squash blossom tattoo revealed? Or if she stayed with his mother in the kitchen, his father would come in and kiss the nape of his mother's neck. His name would be everywhere, breathing in the stairwell, pulsing from the certificates for prizes he had won, and she would not be able to ignore his name with his mother right there. She would silently demand a story about him. She was not ready. What could she say: tango and champagne, the slippery chemises, Carnal Garage, Señor Amor?

At their house she came prepared with a sketchbook and newly sharpened pencils. A soft gray kneaded eraser in her pocket. She did not turn on a light. Sitting in a kitchen chair, her feet on a stool, her knees became an easel, and she drew. Lines were somehow reassuring, predictable. She had always been able to render what was right in front of her. The green tomatoes in their papery husks. The molcajete fashioned from volcanic rock.

She had taken up her pencils. She had entered the art-making trance for half an hour, state of grace he called it. She would leave before his mother came home, ashamed for her to know that she was drawing, that she was alive.

Mariachi had rattled in the street; someone gunned an engine and a motorbike raged.

His father had said, "Bright eyes now." He clicked away for a minute or two. Taking photos of the birthday partiers in a clump under the maple tree.

Mrs. Gonzales said, "Arturo. Time to go to the museum."

Apologetically, his father said, "I'm scheduled to photograph the talent show."

Sophie recalled touching foreheads, his arms around her. Light caught on his St. Chris medal. She thought that they might dance again. Sophie flipped her hair over her shoulder to give him better access to her skin.

She remembered saying, "That's fine, go ahead." He waved and said, "Be right back." He followed his parents and Benny out the side gate.

The disc he burned for her mother's party had gotten around to "Cry Me a River." Three pops out on the street might have been balloons bursting or aborted Cinco de Mayo fireworks. Between the pops and the scream, Mrs. Gonzales wailing, there were perhaps three elastic seconds. Under the orange heat of the braziers and the blue soot shadow of the tree branches, Sophie felt her face break into Cubist sections.

After that it was all disjointed. Shoving people, growling, "*Get*—the *fuck*—out of my way."

Pressing her body against him and coming up bloody. Blood like a butterfly on her white sweater. A policeman rolling up on a Segway.

Mrs. Gonzales, her mouth open in a black O, crying, "Mother of God."

The shrill woow-woow-woow of a siren.

Uncle Leo crouching, his oil-soaked thumb on his forehead.

One of his mother's red pumps lying near his feet.

Mr. Gonzales retching against the bike shop wall, his silver glasses crushed in one hand.

Once last winter, driving home from O'Hare, Sophie beheld a suburban family burying a dog and weeping. It was seven in the morning, the ground hard against their pickax. Their faces slung down, their winter parkas unzipped. She thought of them often: what united all creatures: it pissed her off that we die.

Curiosity like a hard wind finally hustled her out the door. She needed a private life, away from her parents. It was possible to walk the streets and seek out the place that would allow her to speak his name. She would think that she saw him, a tantalizing leather-jacketed shadow around a corner. But she kept going. Her eyes darted covertly left and right; she did not believe the detectives would find his murderer; but her intuition said that a clue might arise on the street, a clue she would treasure and take to the detectives. This was a new stage and she thought: So there will be stages.

Her mother finally left on her trip. Early the next morning, she went to the Dominican priory to visit Uncle Leo. A giraffe-like man, Gandalfian, nearly ninety, Uncle Leo wore his summer uniform, madras shorts and a polo shirt. He met her outside. A handsome red-headed monk in a chalk-colored robe knelt at the sidewalk, planting marigolds from a flat. He and Uncle Leo said hello in the abbreviated way of people who live together, then Uncle Leo patted her back and said, "I wondered when you'd come to see me." They walked around to Jumping Bean, his arm weighty across her shoulder for a block.

Jumping Bean Café was crowded even at that early hour. Yesterday's thrice-read newspapers lay about; posters for loft rentals and political events were taped to the window. On stools at the mosaic counter, they ordered.

He toyed with a book of matches, turning it clockwise with his thumbs, his forefingers. He said, "Do you blame me? For getting him involved?"

"I blame everyone. For everything," she said, shrugging. "I'm sick with blame."

"Come to Mass."

Sophie shrugged again. That was not the direction she was headed.

He told her about his upcoming trial; how he might go to prison for three months. Their family had a subversive history. "If your grandmother hadn't gone into labor with your father, she would've been at the Memorial Day Massacre at Republic Steel." The implication was: When will you get involved? He thought it would be good for her. She had known him a long time; she did not have to hear these things out loud to know that they were true.

You heard the stories of glass and steel workers, McCormick Reaper, meatpacking plants, breweries, railroad workers who were the first to strike in 1877, thirty of them slaughtered by police and the 22nd U.S. infantry, right there in Pilsen. Just as Rudy Lozano was slaughtered in 1983 for organizing labor. His murder remained unsolved. The branch library was named for Rudy Lozano. She had heard the stories but until now—now meaning the last few weeks—the stories had been white noise, an almost inaudible frequency, a name on a building.

In the mirror behind the counter, beyond the salad makings, the stacks of sliced cheese, she noticed their resemblance:

high foreheads, defined chins. The waitress slid their mugs onto the counter. Sophie said, "I think I'm pregnant." She grabbed his gnarly hand, laid her face close to his. His breath smelled like licorice. If she hadn't come out with him, when would she have realized it? She felt slow-witted, with some sort of buffer zone between herself and her bodily reality.

Uncle Leo said, "What a blessing."

And there was the language for it; a blessing. Uncle Leo says it's a blessing, she would tell everyone. A molting had begun; she might shed her mean-spirit like snakeskin.

Benny's studio was in a warren of studios, one mile east of central Pilsen. She trudged there, across the tracks, in the swelter of a June afternoon. She had been circling in her mind for days toward Benny's studio. Discreet signs in the windows announced *digital media* and *urban primitive, fiberglass sculpture* and *etchings.*

A hammer in his hand, Benny in a leather apron leaned over a metal quilt made of flattened pop cans. He offered her a g & t. "First of the summer."

But she said no. She wanted to say, "Why were you going to the museum with his parents? What was it like out on the street? Did he say anything?" There would be time for that, for the acquisition of details. She glanced around the studio: the dogwood out the grimy window, the tea boxes piled helter-skelter. So this is the place. She said, "Luis wanted to move here. He always said, 'Imagine your own sign in the window—Sophie March-Gonzales, Oils.'" It had seemed so far away from home, but now it seemed so close.

Benny slumped in a butterfly chair, his drink on the floor. Traffic hissed on the Dan Ryan.

Sophie said, "I sleep in the living room. On the sofa. But I've been up there. His cigarettes are still on the bedside table. He never smoked indoors and he had this little metal box—it's a little spice box with a sailing ship on it, he bought it at the flea market for a quarter—and he put his cigarette butts in that box. He was kind of a neat freak. He was going to quit. He was. Everything's still there.

His dance shoes. His boots. He always wiped his boots with mink oil. He didn't mind loading the dishwasher, but he didn't like unloading it. Isn't that funny?" She hugged herself as if she were cold and curled up like a fist. She said, "I don't mean funny-funny."

"I know," Benny said. He drank from his g & t and pursed his lips. "It's the shits."

When Benny was a boy he rode in the back of a Buick convertible, with the top down, in a parade to celebrate Eisenhower's second victory. This photograph hung on the wall in his studio. Sophie shook off her tears and got up and peered at the photograph, for something to do. A tyke in a little blazer and tie, Benny waves like the local beauty queen who sits beside him.

Benny got up close to Sophie—she felt a thread of magnetism between them, their arms, which nearly touched. He smelled like gin and brown rice, a clean fusion. The light in the studio was glossy, late afternoon, tinted by the glare of metal trash piled everywhere. "I don't call it trash," he said. "It's ephemera."

It's his grandfather in the driver's seat, he said. A Republican precinct committeeman from downstate, quintessential self-made man, who quit school in second grade and eventually owned a car dealership. The Buick is festooned with crepe paper. There was a quote beneath the photograph.

Every gun that is made, every warship launched, every rocket fired signifies, in the final sense, a theft from those who hunger and are not fed, those who are cold and are not clothed. The world in arms is not spending money alone. It is spending the sweat of its laborers, the genius of its scientists, the hopes of its children...this is not a way of life at all, in any true sense. Under the cloud of threatening war, it is humanity hanging from a cross of iron. April 16, 1953

Sophie said, "Luis would've liked that." It wasn't his name that had been frozen. It was an entire fan of events that lay before her when she spoke his name, like cards of fortune or divination in reverse: a public story she would have to render.

And next to the Eisenhower quote, a poster of radical cheerleaders at a peace march. Lickety-Split and Memphis Dirty Belles, their T-shirts read. Girls in fishnet stockings and cut-off jean skirts, shaking pom-poms made of trash bags.

"My niece there on the far right," Benny said.

"Looks like fun," Sophie said.

"You could probably join up."

She laughed.

Benny set his g & t on a table. He cupped her shoulders and held her at arm's length. With his rough sculptor's hands on her bare shoulders, she thought: Not now but someday. I'll want to speak a new man's name. His face was sunny, brown as a nut; she recalled her father saying that Benny walked miles every morning along the lakeshore, rain or shine, to keep his depression at bay. Apparently, if you didn't want to lose your mind, you had to kick start the effort.

He said, "You laughed."

"I know," she said.

ABOUT THE AUTHOR

 **PATRICIA HENLEY'S**
Hummingbird House was a finalist
for the National Book Award and
the New Yorker Fiction Prize. Her
first collection of stories, *Friday
Night at Silver Star,* was the winner
of the Montana First Book Award
in 1986. The *Chicago Tribune,* the *Seattle Post-Intelligencer,*
and the *St. Louis Dispatch* selected her second novel, *In the
River Sweet,* as one of the best books of 2002. Her stories
have been anthologized in *Best American Short Stories, The
Pushcart Prize* anthology, *The Last Best Place, Love Stories for
the Rest of Us,* and *The Art of the Short Story.* Her published
works include two novels, four collections of stories, two
chapbooks of poetry, and numerous essays. She teaches in
the MFA Program in Creative Writing at Purdue University.

CPSIA information can be obtained at www.ICGtesting.com
Printed in the USA
LVOW081758260912

300440LV00011B/7/P